FINISH!
Leveraging career, sport, faith and failure

E. ZeNai Brooks, CPA

PUBLISHING

FINISH!

© Copyright 2021 E. ZeNai Brooks

All rights reserved. This book is protected by the copyright laws of the United States of America. Its contents and or cover may not be copied or reprinted in whole or in part, stored in a retrieval system or transmitted to any form or by any means: electronic, mechanical, photocopy, recording or any other form for any commercial or media use, gain or profit. The use of short quotations, occasional minimal page copying for personal or group study is permitted.

FINISH!
Leveraging career, sport, faith and failure

Published by:
ATK PUBLISHING
8401 Moller Rd. Ste. 68244
Indianapolis, IN 46268
atkspf.com | atkpublishing@gmail.com

ISBN: 9781732417496

FOREWORD

INTRODUCTION   1

CHAPTER 1 | *DISCIPLINES OF COMPLETION*   12

    DISCIPLINE 1 | GOAL SETTING 15
    DISCIPLINE 2 | MOTIVATION 20
    DISCIPLINE 3 | DISCIPLINE 24
    DISCIPLINE 4 | PERSEVERANCE 30
    DISCIPLINE 5 | FAITH 36

CHAPTER 2 | *COMMIT*   41

    COMMIT TO A PLAN 45
    COMMIT TO THE PROCESS 49
    COMMIT TO LEARNING 56

CHAPTER 3 | *DISTRACTIONS*   62

    THE LAW OF DISTRACTION 64
    SHIFT FOCUS 67
    F.O.M.O 70
    MAKE TIME, NOT EXCUSES 77

CHAPTER 4 | *RECOMMIT*   90

    LEARN FROM FAILING 93
    ASK FOR HELP 99
    GIVE YOURSELF GRACE 106

CHAPTER 5 | *FINISH*   116

    START BY STARTING 122
    ESTABLISH PURPOSEFUL BOUNDARIES 129
    FINISH! 137

CONCLUSION 142

CALL TO ACTION 145
SUCCESS 149
SIGNIFICANCE 155

TOOLS 159

KEYS STEPS TO FINISH 159
ENCOURAGING NOTES TO SELF 160
Z'S ZINGERS TO REMEMBER 161
PERSONAL REALIZATIONS 163

ABOUT THE AUTHOR

ABOUT ATKSP FIRM

Foreword

There are no words to express the excitement I felt when ZeNai shared her plans with me to write this book. I was even more ecstatic when she approached me about writing the foreword for the book. If you haven't guessed by the last name, ZeNai and I have been married seven and half years and I was right there with her throughout much of the process which she speaks about in this book. I am the proud Senior Pastor of the New Liberty Missionary Baptist Church of Indianapolis, Indiana, and a National Gospel Recording Artist. Yes, this means ZeNai serves as the Pastor's wife, First Lady of the Church, Financial Secretary, my personal Booking Manager, and many other duties stemming from her experience, skills, and leadership training.

When ZeNai and I married, I knew that God blessed me with a "special" young lady, but over the past seven years, God has shown me just how special she is. I watched her take on major projects at work, Church, the National Association of Black Accountants (NABA), The Indianapolis Urban League Exchange (Young Professionals) and maintain a consistent CrossFit routine, and, yes, I said "CrossFit". All while studying to pass all four parts of the CPA exam. She and I both manage very busy schedules, but we do it differently. There are times when I look at her and ask, "How do you do it?" Well, she provides the answers to that question in this book.

Although I felt honored to be asked to write this foreword, I initially thought it should be written by one of her mentors or someone in the profession. After prayerful consideration, I decided there is no one better to write this than me. I watched her and took care of her throughout this process. I prayed with her just before every test. I cooked for her when she needed extra study time. I encouraged her when she missed passing a portion of the exam by one or two points. There are others who may be qualified to write this foreword, but there are none more deserving of this great honor. Imagine a typical day in the life of the Brooks Family while "Z" was preparing for an exam (Study regimen started, examine already scheduled, etc.). Let's use a typical Tuesday. She wakes up at 5 a.m., go to the gym for a workout or outside for a run, back home by 7 a.m., packs my lunch for work, showers, joins my weekly 7 a.m. prayer call, gets dressed and heads to work, works all day, meets me at Church for midweek Bible Study, orders dinner, picks it up on the way home, has dinner with me, and then retreats to the office to study at about 8 p.m. until about 10 or 11 p.m. The very next day she does it all over again. I gave you an example of one day, but what if I told you this is what her day looked like almost every day? I watched her adjust her schedule to begin studying in the mornings while I was still sleep. I watched her get back on the horse after not passing an exam. I watched her juggle so many aspects of life as she preserved with discipline towards her goal. ZeNai was able to "manage" a busy life and still do the necessary work to finish what she started.

Is this book for you? Only you can answer that. Do you have unfinished business? Do you have difficult tasks you need to complete? Do you have ambitious goals? And more importantly, do you have the drive needed to complete said tasks? If you answered yes to any of these questions and you are simply looking for guidance on where and how to FINISH!; this book is indeed for you.

Humbly submitted,

Pastor Darrell L. Brooks
Proud Husband

FINISH!

INTRODUCTION

INTRODUCTION

Don't you love when your eyes open before your alarm actually goes off? Especially when it feels like you closed them just minutes ago. This is me before major events, including big games, speaking engagements, and even taking exams. I've always tried to pull all-nighters before an exam, but for probably obvious reasons, my brain would stop comprehending material after midnight. So here I am, lying in bed, after three hours of sleep, wide-awake, googling whether it's a good idea to study ("cram") on the day of your exam.

> *"If I get up now, I can review practice test questions again for an hour and then review simulations for another hour. Then I can stop at Starbucks for more coffee and a protein box, and arrive at the test site an hour early and cram a little more"*

1

FINISH! *INTRODUCTION*

    Why would I need to cram the morning of the exam when I've been studying for months? Because, I have tried and failed this exam more than I would like to admit. Between 2008 and 2020, I had applied for sections of the CPA exam over 20 times; only passing one section. At this point it was clear to me I was not a good test taker, my memory sucked, and it was possible I was simply not as smart as I thought I was. These disparaging thoughts and feelings of doubt, insecurity, and imposter syndrome weighed on me and plagued my mind for the better part of 12 years.

"I can't do this.
Maybe I'm not really that smart.
Do I have a learning disability?
I'm pretty sure I have ADHD.
Have I been overhyped my entire life?
Do I need to change careers?
Why does this seem so easy for everyone else?
Lord, what's wrong with me?"

FINISH! *INTRODUCTION*

After graduating college in 2008 and beginning a career in public accounting at one of the Big 4 accounting firms, I decided to obtain the CPA license. Actually, it was decided for me. Obtaining the Certified Public Accountant (CPA) license was not an initial dream or goal of mine. To me, it is a pseudo requirement to advance as an accountant in certain careers. Sitting for the CPA exam is similar to the requirement of doctors to pass the Boards and lawyers to pass the Bar. The one caveat is one can still practice accounting or tax and be successful without actually obtaining the license. For me, this was problem number 1: why do certain organizations employing accounting, finance and tax professionals use the CPA license as a measurement or barrier of entry? Problem number 2: the pass rate for each of the four exams required to pass to obtain the CPA license ranges between 45 and 55%. Effectively making this license more difficult to obtain than both the previously mentioned doctor and lawyer credentials. I'll go over the benefits of the CPA

FINISH! *INTRODUCTION*

license a bit later. However, understand that I am both an advocate and critic of this licensing process: I'll save that for a different platform.

To give you a full picture of the magnitude of this certification, I will explain the process. In order to obtain the CPA license, you must pass a series of business-related exams, collectively known as the CPA exam. The four parts are:

- Financial Accounting and Reporting (FAR) - all things accounting
- Business Environment and Concepts (BEC) - all things business including economics, governance, and information technology
- Regulation (REC) - all things tax including business law and ethics
- Audit and Attestation - all things risk, controls, and processes

Each part is taken separately, but one must pass all of them within a span of 18 months. They can be taken in any order, but the clock starts once the first one is passed: note I said passed not when you take the first one. Each part is four hours. The

FINISH! *INTRODUCTION*

test includes multiple choice questions, simulations, and written memos (only BEC). Each exam cost approximately $250 to register, with an additional $85 registration fee in Indiana. Problem number 3: remember the test has a pretty low pass rate, so cost start to add up.

One other *little* thing to point out: less than 2% of all CPAs are Black. That's fewer than Black doctors, engineers, and lawyers who represent approximately 5% of their population. According to the most recent census conducted by the US Census Bureau, Black people make up 13.4% of the United States population. Here in lies Problem number 4.

<u>Perception is not always...</u>

Now, back to me. Why am I doing this? A lingering question I definitively could not answer. Why? Because for every justifiable, proven benefit of taking the CPA exam; I had a counter argument or rationalization. This over-analysis wasn't helpful; it was actually counterproductive. After 12 years, I spent more time talking myself out of completing the CPA exam than actually studying for it. Talk about wasted energy! (Zing!) The way I saw it, or the way others perceived it, between 2008 and 2020, I had begun to make a name for myself. I had a seemingly successful and stable career. I served on local and national not-for-profit boards, including committees and task forces that actually advocated for the CPA license. I had also become the First Lady of a church (yes, a pastor's wife). I had started preaching and teaching the Bible and launched a religious blog. I found a way to stay fit by competing in local volleyball leagues, doing CrossFit, and even completing in four Spartan races. I had a full schedule. Yes, Problem 5.

    This is where imposter syndrome kicks in, which according to Google is loosely defined as doubting your abilities and feeling like a fraud. The perception others had of me was: "ZeNai has a good life, good career, good influence, good reputation, good exposure, and makes good money." To me, none of this was *good* enough. All of this was overshadowed by the exam failures that weighed on my conscious and confidence. In 2020, I started and stopped five serious attempts of the Exam process. Over 20 times, I had taken 'not-so-serious' attempts at various parts of the exam; resulting in me passing only one part! Yes, one!

In addition to the blow to my self-esteem, my pockets took a financial hit. Even with companies helping to cover part of the cost of the exam and study materials, it was a lot to absorb. I was SO SICK of this process. I wanted to quit. I was tired of talking about it. I was tired of thinking about it. I was tired of explaining it. Quitting would be much easier. People would eventually forget that I tried and failed, right? Maybe? But I knew I wouldn't. (Zing!)

Moment of Truth

While I seemed to have my stuff together, if I'm honest, my career wasn't progressing in the way it should have. While I'd gained great knowledge and experience through my career moves, I had made a series of semi lateral moves. This was, in part, an effort to avoid or escape the ghost of the CPA license and to buy myself additional time. You see, if I really wanted to be a partner at a CPA firm or a high-level executive, the rules say I needed the license. I watched people that were younger than me and with less experience be promoted. I saw people that began their careers at the same time as me move to higher level positions. I remember getting denied for job opportunities. And it was not because I didn't have the skills or experience (note: I was actually overqualified professionally and technically), but because I did not possess the pseudo qualifier of the CPA credential.

    I couldn't go out like that. After 12 years and now with my back against the wall, the answer to the aforementioned lingering question, "Why am I doing this?" ultimately became:

FINISH! INTRODUCTION

> *Because I have to*
> *Because I started it*
> *Because I'm a winner, not a quitter*
>   *(I actually have championships)*
> *Because I cannot be a hypocrite*
> *Because I am actually smart*
> *Because I am a badass*
> *Because I want to be an example for others*
> *Because I want to increase representation of underrepresented people, especially Black women*
> *Because I can change the rules, from the inside*

Somewhere between deciding for myself that I wanted this license, and the necessity to advance in my career, I finally tapped into my own discipline and found the secret sauce to FINISH! what I started and complete the CPA exam. This is what I will share with you in this book. The secret sauce was inside me the whole time; the secret sauce that drove success in many areas of my life. The secret sauce was not actually a secret; I had been preparing, practicing, and using it my entire life. I simply had to figure out how to apply the sauce to this part of my life and execute the process. Leveraging the same disciplines I used for my career, my sport, and my faith was what was needed for me to FINISH! the CPA exam.

Whether you are seeking to obtain your CPA license, pass the bar exam, pass the boards, obtain a master's degree, finish a book, start a business, or complete a marathon race, this book is for you! There are a lot of people suffering in silence on how to FINISH! and the disappointment of not. Let's change that narrative and remove the stigma and embarrassment of failure. I pray that being transparent about my experiences, epiphanies, successes, best practices, and my failures will help you push pass procrastination, fear, and doubt to reach the goals you have established for yourself! And if you have not defined your goals, this book will help you do that as well!

In order to FINISH what you have started; you must commit to discipline and perseverance. It

FINISH! *INTRODUCTION*

will push you to the FINISH line, just like it did for me!

> **ZeNai** @LadyZSpeaks
> When you are committed to discipline and perseverance, you can FINISH! what you have started!
>
> #ZsZingers #ladyzspeaks #finish

Throughout each chapter you will find "Z's Zingers". These are tweetable, bite-sized; striking remarks and outstanding thoughts that can be shared on social media! Do share and be sure to tag #finish! #ZsZingers #ladyzspeaks

FINISH!

Chapter 1

Chapter 1 | *Disciplines of Completion*

I was a college athlete. And by this, I mean scholarship athlete at the University of Louisville; where in my senior year, my track team won the Big East Championship. This was a significant improvement from placing last in Conference USA during my freshman year. Leading the charge that championship year, I placed first in the Hammer throw and 6th in the Shot Put. In the last three years of my five-year collegiate athlete career, between indoor and outdoor shot put, indoor weight throw, and outdoor hammer throw, I racked up 7 first place finishes and 15 other top 3 finishes. I like to think my college career was pretty impressive for an undersized thrower from Indiana who only as a third sport option didn't start track until her freshman year in high school. Now this type of success and overall team improvements did not happen overnight. It was a result of waking up at 5am for weight training, going to class during the day, and practicing again at 4pm for 9 months out of the year for 5 years. This type of success was a result of practicing outside in the rain and snow and freezing temperatures when we didn't have an indoor facility. When I think about it, this type of success started way before I entered college.

I have a strong foundation when it comes to structure. My parents were hyper focused on making sure my two siblings and I not only had what we needed physically, but they made sure we had a routine so we could complete all of our tasks and accomplish our goals. I started playing sports in elementary school at the YMCA. By the time I graduated high school, I was a three-sport athlete, playing club volleyball (during school basketball season) and AAU basketball (during school track season). In addition, while taking AP classes, I was a class officer, student council and national honor society member.

With all these activities, my parents; especially my mom, ran a tight ship. Here is what

FINISH!   *Disciplines of Completion*

a typical day was like: Wake up at 6am. School drop off by 7:15am. School pickup from practice by 5:30pm. Homework until 7pm. Dinner and family jeopardy until 8pm. Bedtime. Sleep. Wake up. Do it again. This routine, which seems impossible these days, was the beginning of the foundation to a successful college career and fundamental to the person I am today.

Achieving the success of passing the CPA exam is a result of this foundation and implementing what I've determined as my secret sauce: Z's principles of completion which include goal setting, motivation, discipline, perseverance, and faith. I realized these same disciplines that guided me to success in other areas of my life, needed to be applied to get me through the CPA Exam. (Zing!)

FINISH!   *Disciplines of Completion*

Discipline 1 | *Goal Setting*

The process of identifying something you want to accomplish and establishing measurable targets and timeframes

"Goal-setting meaning | Best 1 definitions of goal-setting," 2020

While it's normal for one's goal to change as you grow, evolve, and gain additional experience, we should ensure that whatever goal we have, the goal is actually ours and we actually believe it. Being 100% sold on the goal, or at least 75% will increase your chance of reaching the goal in a timely manner. If you determine you are not really interested in said goal, you will never achieve it.

My initial plan in high school was to become an engineer. Not because I actually wanted to be an engineer or build or create things. But since I took classes like AP Physics and AP Calculus, my teachers, counselors, parents, and the career assessment test determined I met the professional profile of an engineer. I tend to be an optimist, seeing the glass half full and becoming a

FINISH! *Disciplines of Completion*

chameleon in most situations. This is a great attribute to have, except when it comes to being decisive. I used to have a hard time making concrete decisions, because I could literally make the most out of any situation. So, I entered college, majoring in Mechanical Engineering, because that's what everyone said I should do. After a semester of Computer Algebra for Engineering and Engineering Analysis; based on my grades, I was obviously not interested in these classes or the major. I knew this career choice wasn't for me. But what did I want to do? Not sure still, I just needed to retain my math credits, which would transfer nicely to the business school. At this juncture, I remembered taking an accounting class during high school and I was pretty good at it. This is where the idea of being an accountant was born.

Fun Fact: I also minored in Sports Administration. My initial goal was not to become a CPA or an accountant. Fast forward five years of college and twelve years of professional experience, the goal

FINISH! *Disciplines of Completion*

was again set for me. Much like high school, given my education and experience, the expectation was that I would go on to obtain the CPA license. Me not being 100% vested in this process ultimately led to me dragging completion of my obtaining my license.

> **ZeNai** @LadyZSpeaks
> It's okay if you back door the goal, if it is not your initial intent. But you must commit to the process to achieve it!
>
> #ZsZingers #ladyzspeaks #finish

FINISH!   *Disciplines of Completion*

Writing Prompt:

What goal are you aiming to achieve?

_____

_____

_____

_____

_____

_____

_____

_____

_____

_____

_____

_____

FINISH!   *Disciplines of Completion*

Writing Prompt:

Is this a goal you have always wanted or was it decided for you?

_____

_____

_____

_____

_____

_____

_____

_____

_____

_____

_____

Discipline 2 | *Motivation*

The reasons why you are doing something, or the level of desire you have to do something - yourdictionary.com

A popular phrase today says, "Motivation gets you started, and discipline keeps you going." I wholeheartedly believe this with one caveat: motivation must be derived from clear internal values. (Zing!) Motivation should not be determined by external factors. Motivation must come from one's internal desire to achieve success.

After 12 years of fighting with the CPA exam, it was clear that my motivation was misplaced and not firmly rooted. I was forced to reconsider my goals, my actions, and my purpose; after which, my motivation became extremely clear. I was no longer on the fence or questioning my objective or beholden to outside expectations. I became motivated by the desire for completion (needing to FINISH what I started), career advancement (to be promoted at work and achieve longer term

FINISH!   *Disciplines of Completion*

executive seats) and a purpose bigger than me (to increase the number of underrepresented people with the license).

Once you determine your goal, solidify it by documenting your "why". Even if it changes and evolves into a deeper purpose, you must be clear on the "what" and the why. This should be driven by your own core values. Without this type of motivation, it is difficult and seemingly impossible to stay on a path towards achievement, especially without wasting time.

> **ZeNai** @LadyZSpeaks
> Motivation is targeted to obtain a goal. Discipline is the driver to FINISH! it.
>
> #ZsZingers #ladyzspeaks #finish

FINISH! *Disciplines of Completion*

Writing Prompt:

What is currently motivating you to get started towards your goal?

_____

_____

_____

_____

_____

_____

_____

_____

_____

_____

_____

FINISH! *Disciplines of Completion*

Writing Prompt:

What influences your motivation and how has that changed?

_____

_____

_____

_____

_____

_____

_____

_____

_____

_____

_____

FINISH! *Disciplines of Completion*

<u>Discipline 3 | *Discipline*</u>

To train or develop by instruction and exercise especially in self-control - merriam-webster.com

A universal truth society has come to agree on, is that sports help to develop key skills which help young people succeed. Even as an uber competitive person, always wanting to win and having big goals, this truth was not initially evident to me. It didn't dawn on me until late in my high school athletic career that some people were not playing sports to obtain college scholarships. Some people were not playing sports to play professionally. Some parents actually encouraged their children to play sports solely for the non-physical, non-professional benefits that sports provides.

Participating in sport encourages teamwork and develops the ability to get along with others. Participating in sports also promotes leadership skills, resilience, increases self-esteem, mental and physical health, and of course, discipline.

FINISH!   *Disciplines of Completion*

Discipline includes having to show up on time for practice, having to rest the night before games, having to consistently plan and think ahead, having to balance being a student and an athlete, and much more. Note: these same disciplines can also be the result of being involved in activities outside of sport (i.e., music, art, clubs, etc.). I've learned to appreciate sport as the "great equalizer". Regardless of one's background, regardless of if you agree with your teammate and regardless of their views off the court, sport has a way of bringing people together for one common goal: to win. Winning becomes the equalizer. Being successful as a team can be the motivation that builds bridges and breaks barriers.

    Being able to balance the increasing responsibilities of life, whether it be sport, music, arts, politics, etc., will always develop and strengthen fundamental skills that can help achieve success in other areas of life. Being able to stay consistent in working towards a goal and persevere through obstacles builds discipline.

FINISH! *Disciplines of Completion*

Discipline will take you places that motivation alone cannot to keep or sustain you.

> **ZeNai** @LadyZSpeaks
> The key to goal achievement is having the ability to cross functionally apply discipline.
>
> #ZsZingers #ladyzspeaks #finish

FINISH!   *Disciplines of Completion*

Writing Prompt:

In what areas of your life are you most disciplined?

_____
_____
_____
_____
_____
_____
_____
_____
_____
_____
_____
_____

FINISH! *Disciplines of Completion*

Writing Prompt:

In what areas of your life do you struggle to be disciplined?

_____

_____

_____

_____

_____

_____

_____

_____

_____

_____

_____

FINISH! *Disciplines of Completion*

Writing Prompt:

What actions can you implement to increase your discipline?

_____
_____
_____
_____
_____
_____
_____
_____
_____
_____
_____
_____

FINISH! *Disciplines of Completion*

Discipline 4 | *Perseverance*

The quality that allows someone to continue trying to do something even though it is difficult - merriam-webster.com

We live in a time my husband likes to call the "microwave society". This term comes from being able to cook food quickly in the microwave or air fryer, instead of waiting for the longer cooking process of the oven or slow cooker. Thanks to Amazon, Instacart, Uber, and other convenient delivery services, we have fewer wait times and less hassle; we can access almost anything in a moment's notice. As a result, we tend to have lower levels of patience and an increased need for instant gratification. In many situations, however, fast is not always best or attainable. Doing the hard things in life literally require us to slow walk through the process. (Zing!)

You may not fully understand the sport of track and field but believe me when I say it's one of the longest sporting events ever. Not only the day of the event, but the preparation and training that lead up to track season. In college, we had the indoor season, which started in December and an outdoor season, which started in March. It was never ending, seemingly a year-round sport. Additionally, with the NCAA Championships held in June, we didn't get much of a summer break before starting weightlifting and training to start the season all over again. With the season so far away, practicing in late summer and early fall seemed trivial and meaningless. However, the long training period allowed our bodies to endure growth and development, peaks and valleys, with the consistent practice embedding our technique to set in. This discipline of training and preparation was crucial to our success and developing perseverance.

>*Fun Fact:* I ended up attending college for 5 years. Not because I wanted to obtain an additional degree or credit hours but because I had an additional year of athletic eligibility. Actually, all the throwers on the track team did. The summer between my

freshman and sophomore year was a turning point for our track program. Our teams went from having a separate men and women's team, with separate coaching staff, to having a combined team with shared coaches. Our new throwing coach accepted the position, I assume, with one caveat, that he would have an opportunity to retrain us. This meant that my sophomore was a redshirt year. In college athletics, this means that athletes extend their eligibility by not competing competitively for the year. Yes, that meant that for a full year, we practiced. We practiced and did not complete in one scored track meet. A long track season became even longer, but we persevered, and it paid off. As a team, we went from being the worst team in Conference USA athletic conference in 2004, to placing top 10 in the Big East athletic conference in 2006, with many of us winning individual events throughout the year. Winning and seeing the

FINISH! *Disciplines of Completion*

success of our hard work was very rewarding. This experience also caused us to grow as teammates but also friends.

> **ZeNai** @LadyZSpeaks
> If you learn to enjoy the journey, it won't seem as painful.
>
> #ZsZingers #ladyzspeaks #finish

FINISH! *Disciplines of Completion*

Writing Prompt:

Has there been a time when you've had to persevere longer than you expected?

_____

_____

_____

_____

_____

_____

_____

_____

_____

_____

_____

_____

FINISH!   *Disciplines of Completion*

Writing Prompt:

What helps you stay focused on your goals?

_____

_____

_____

_____

_____

_____

_____

_____

_____

_____

_____

_____

FINISH! *Disciplines of Completion*

Discipline 5 | *Faith*

The quality that allows someone to continue trying to do something even though it is difficult - merriam-webster.com

"I can do all things through Christ which strengthens me." (Phil 4:13) This has been my favorite Scripture for as long as I can remember. I often use it as the answer when I am asked how to balance everything I have going on. I consider it an acknowledgment that by myself, I cannot accomplish anything. I must fully rely on Christ to give me the secret sauce: the motivation, the discipline and the perseverance to be successful and reach my goals. Being able to rely on Christ relieves me of the pressure of having to be perfect, having to be the smartest, having imposter syndrome, and even having to make decisions on my own.

Making a decision to choose faith is more than words, it centers on action and is evident by the way you navigate life. Faith isn't the absence of anxiety or fear. Faith to me is the ability to act, with hope, in spite of anxiety and fear. Faith, as explained in the Bible, is the substance of things hoped for and the evidence of things not seen (Hebrews 11:1). This means, faith is the tool we can use to "do it scared". While faith may not look pretty because things are falling apart, we cannot see what the end will be, and we feel as if we are behind, believing that God is still in control is critical part of goal achievement.

Even when you appear to be behind, I encourage you to wait on God! Even when others rush us, when all appears lost, when we get impatient or discouraged... we must learn to wait on God and have faith in the process! It may not be ideal in your mind but know that God can and will redeem your time!

> **ZeNai** @LadyZSpeaks
> Allowing Christ to be my center and my focus disciplines me for success!
>
> #ZsZingers #ladyzspeaks #finish

FINISH!   *Disciplines of Completion*

Writing Prompt:

How easy or difficult is it for you to apply faith in tough situations?

_____

_____

_____

_____

_____

_____

_____

_____

_____

_____

_____

_____

FINISH! *Disciplines of Completion*

Writing Prompt:

What role does faith play in your daily life?

_____

_____

_____

_____

_____

_____

_____

_____

_____

_____

_____

FINISH! *Disciplines of Completion*

Writing Prompt:

Can you remember a difficult time where you have had to apply faith? How did that work out?

_____

_____

_____

_____

_____

_____

_____

_____

_____

_____

_____

_____

FINISH!

Chapter 2

Chapter 2 | *Commit*

My journey committing to the CPA exam was a long one, with lots of starts and restarts along the way. Part of the elongated twelve-year journey was committing to the commitment, committing to the process and committing to perseverance. My reality is, I had never had to intentionally practice commitment on my own. I had never had to work this hard to remove distractions. I had always been part of a system, part of structure that was already laid out for me. All I had to do was show up. Growing up my parents gave us routine. Along my high school and college careers, I maintained routine. Even after graduating college, as a professional, it seemed like being structured and routine was embedded in my DNA, at least when it came to sport.

For as long as I can remember, I have been known to wake up early to work out. I remember living in downtown Indianapolis, waking up at 4:30 to attend boot camp 25 minutes away in Zionsville,

IN. I would set out my workout clothes at night and pack my work clothes so I could shower and change in the locker room at my job. I even keep a routine, or tight schedule, when it comes to my community and church commitments. My Gmail calendar is always current with upcoming events, meetings, deadlines and even blocking out time to work out, read, study and anything else I need to remember to do. This all stemmed from my built-in system of structure that developed over time as a result of my years of operating on a calendar and deadline driven schedule. I jokingly refer to myself as a "machine" because of the way I operate purposely throughout life. Unlike people who need a little more flexibility, I actually enjoyed the rigorous lifestyle. I never experienced burn out or regret because I genuinely enjoyed the activities, the sport and the people I was surrounded by.

That said, part of my frustration with the CPA exam journey was that none of the routine and structure I implemented worked. Why did my planning and OCD tendencies work in every other aspect of my life, except this area? Simple answer. I was not truly invested and the journey was not enjoyable or rewarding. In hindsight, I realize I was also not as committed to passing the exam as I was to being an athlete, being a good board member or being a good church leader. The CPA license took the back seat to everything else I was doing and wanted to do. The CPA license got the leftovers of my time, focus, and energy. I needed to prioritize my CPA studies, just like I did in my commitment to sport. Once I understood how to apply my previous practices of committing to sport to my studies, I was able to tailor a plan to overcome the CPA exam.

In 2018, I began to proactively practice discipline. I came up with a strategy to practice sacrifice. It was an exercise in telling myself, "No". My discipline tended to stem from external factors like being coached or because someone else was watching. But could I become better at self-discipline? Could I practice discipline when no one was looking and frankly when no one else cared?

FINISH!　　　　　　　　　　　　*Commit*

I needed to train my brain to weigh options differently and according to priorities. I also needed a system to help minimize my decision-making and brain fatigue. I created a system of discipline. Each month I would place one item of food or beverage on the restricted list. I would rotate items each month, trying to avoid repeating. This barrier set a clear boundary of what I needed to avoid. Overtime, I became unbothered by the restriction which was a surprising result. It was getting easier to respect the boundaries I created for myself. I considered this my kickoff to the self-discipline I needed on the CPA exam journey. Telling myself "No" to certain foods or drinks, developed a muscle that helped me to tell myself No in other areas. Sticking to this exercise of discipline allowed me to stay focused on the big picture. This was also an exercise of sacrifice which interrupted the feeling of missing out and distraction.

In researching for this book, I discovered this is a common practice people implement when they want to refocus. I am not sure if this actually increased my scores on the CPA exam, but I know for a fact this exercise helped me to develop the mental toughness necessary to stay committed to the journey.

> **ZeNai** @LadyZSpeaks
> Many people fail to reach their goals because they do not stick to the plan...or have a plan!
>
> #ZsZingers #ladyzspeaks #finish

Commit to a Plan

We have all heard the old adage, "If you fail to plan, you are failing to plan." This should be the foundation of one's decision for goal setting. If you do not have a plan, it is very likely that either you will not (ever) reach your goal or it will take you a really long time; much longer than necessary. Think about it. As a championship athlete, I practiced according to a plan. Not only showing up to practice and weight training daily, but also the actual training schedule that was developed to promote growth and development. To increase strength and peak at the right time, I had a specific weight-training regime that I followed closely. I had a specific practice schedule that focused on breaking down the throwing technique early in the season then pulling it all together during the tournament. I used every practice and track meet as an opportunity to assess, reassess, and adjust the training plan. Randomly showing up to practice and weightlifting with no clear direction or assessment would not have resulted in success.

Having structure and a plan are key factors in achieving any goal; whether the goal is sport related or not. Even our education system is set up like this. Lessons are broken down over semesters and terms in order to ensure that each student grows in knowledge and application through the year(s). Many students fail classes because they do not stick to the structured plan.

Creating a plan is major key! And not just any plan, a realistic plan. Many people swear by

FINISH! *Commit*

the SMART method when it comes to goal setting The SMART method involves setting goals that are Specific, Measurable, Attainable, Relevant (or Realistic), and Time-Bound. ("There's a S.M.A.R.T. way to write management's goals and objectives." Management Review. 70 (11): 35–36.)

SMART Considerations:

Specific: Are you clear about the who, what, when, where and why?

Measurable: How will you determine the milestones and progress?

Attainable: Are you in a position and have met the criteria to achieve the goal?

Relevant (Realistic): Does this goal align with your life's purpose?

Timebound: When will you complete the goal?

Using these criteria to set your goals only works if you develop a plan and boundaries to support the goal. When I say create a realistic plan, I mean create a plan that matches your personality, your budget, your attention span,

FINISH! *Commit*

learning style, and even your interest. One mistake I initially made was using a standard studying plan that wasn't a good fit for me. I wasted so much time forcing myself to watch 2-3 hours worth of lectures after work instead of reading the book myself or doing multiple-choice questions; I had to learn my learning style. I stressed myself by cutting out social time and workouts, instead of incorporating self-care into my learning process; I had to learn the importance of balance. Lastly, I pressured myself to study according to the prescribed timeline instead of considering my work and personal commitments; I had to learn to incorporate aspects of my life instead of excluding them.

> **ZeNai** @LadyZSpeaks
> Your plan of action must line up with goals and personality if you are going to FINISH!
>
> #ZsZingers #ladyzspeaks #finish

FINISH! *Commit*

Having a better understanding how to create a realistic plan that is specific to you and your goal will definitely increase your chances of achieving your goal.

Commit to the Process

Several years ago, my husband and I had the opportunity to hear Former U.S Secretary of State, Commander Colin Powell speak at a local event. His speech was meant to encourage the audience in personal success and empower us to be engaged in community. One statement he made resonated with both my husband and me. In defining the art of war, which was the basis of his motivation, your approach begins with "examining all possible options by committee to determine the best option. Once you determine the best option, you must execute it violently". What I heard was "Whatever your end goal is, determine the best path to get there. The execute it violently!" Ever since then, we have used this approach as a guiding light to goal setting, living on purpose, and being more intentional in general. The reality is that a goal is only as good as the action you are willing to put into it. And if you are not willing to intentionally attack it, you may miss achieving said goal. Once you set a plan, you must be willing to implement the plan as well as endure through the ups, downs, and changes in the process. No matter how long it takes, you have to stay the course because veering off track only causes additional delays. This is totally how I ended up taking 12 years to FINISH the CPA exam. I was not committed to all aspects of the process. I wanted to obtain the CPA license, but I was not fully committed to the ups and downs of the journey. I am honestly not sure why I was not committed but there were definitely not any violent attacks to get there happening. Instead, this thing was attacking me. Mentally and emotionally! So, I created a defense mechanism to save me, for me to avoid disappointment, failure, and embarrassment. This journey was not easy or natural to me; it was hard.

I was not willing to commit too much energy into the process. I expected to FINISH this exam with a smooth journey, but I hadn't determined a plan to violently attack this goal.

By committing to a goal, which is a particularly important step, you must understand what comes with the process. You must understand the full scope of the process to ensure that you have what it takes to follow through. And if you realize you may not have what it takes, determine whether you have what it takes to develop? See, this process of committing involves sacrifice, it involves dedication, it involves discipline, and it involves patience. It involves the willingness to grow; which occurs along the journey. We tend to rush through the process of growth and development but doing so does not fully equip us for success. We must acknowledge

FINISH! *Commit*

patience as an integral part of commitment, closely coupled with its cousin, perseverance.

> **ZeNai** @LadyZSpeaks
> If we are prepared for the bumps, they will be easier to attack once they arrive.
>
> #ZsZingers #ladyzspeaks #finish

Fun Fact: I randomly signed up for a Spartan Race a couple of years ago. Spartan races vary in length, but the first one I did was approximately 4 miles with 20 obstacles along the way. This means running through the hills, woods, sand, and mud around the Perfect North Ski Resort in Southern, IN, while having to jump over walls, climb ropes, carry 35-pound sandbags and more. The craziest part of my first race was that not only was it over 100 degrees out that day, the very first obstacle was running up what seemed like a 45-degree hill, which felt like it was a mile long.

Several people were taken out on that first obstacle. When I say taken out, I mean laying down on the hill, trying to catch their breath. The race was intense right off the bat. I managed to keep going, one foot in front of the other, even as my run became a jog and then a fast walk. Throughout the race, all I could think was to keep going. If I stopped, I would never FINISH, so just keep going.

I believe that every person that showed up for the race had the same mindset. Every person was prepared to keep going; to endure the heat, the hills and all the obstacles. Every person that showed up was committed to perseverance. Even though we knew there would be obstacles to deal with along the way, we didn't know exactly what they would look like, we just knew that we would FINISH, one way or another. We knew that we had to persevere, but we also knew we had to be patient. There was no sprinting our way through this Spartan race. Trying to hurry and get to the end would surely backfire and cause you to not make it at all. (Seriously. We saw people getting carried out of the course, on stretchers because they were going too fast, too hard and maybe were not prepared.) Sprinting is running full speed for a short period of time and is not sustainable for longer periods of time. In most things in life, I am a sprinter (do not confuse this with being a thrower in college); I like to get things done fast and in shorter burst. Obtaining my CPA license was a long-distance race though, much like the Spartan Race, which requires both perseverance and patience.

Perseverance I could do, patience, however, has never been my strong suit. As much as I pray for it, God answers me in ways that I did (and do) not necessarily enjoy. He continues to give me more opportunities to put this skill of patience into action. I am now convinced that this

CPA journey was one of those skill tests. A step further, it has been a test of my ability to endure and to persevere; a test of my sheer ability to weather the storm. It was a test for me to recognize the prayers that God had answered and an opportunity for me to put into practice all the skills I learned through sport, family, and my career. It was an opportunity for me to tap into the process of preparation that God was leading me towards.

Unfortunately, I, like many others, gave up too fast. We get discouraged. We get detoured. We try to sprint and rush through the process. None of these are avoidable, but if allowed, they can throw us off track. Just remember, things may not always go as smoothly as you plan for, but the bumps are also part of the process that we must accept, commit to and patiently persevere. Zing!

FINISH! *Commit*

Commit to Learning

Sit down and be humble!

When I arrived on campus at the University of Louisville as a thrower, I had experience in high school at throwing shot put, discus and weight training. However, I had no experience with throwing the hammer. The wrong thing to do would have been to assume that I knew how to throw the hammer, simply because I knew how to throw the shot put and the discus (which I didn't actually throw the discus in college). I had to be willing to learn this new throw and be humble enough to listen to the coach.

While I could leverage certain aspects of my previous experience, there were certain nuisances specific to the hammer throw that I had no understanding of. Long story short, I became better at throwing the hammer than the shot put,

FINISH! Commit

but it required that I first commit to learning the technique.

> **ZeNai** @LadyZSpeaks
> As we set new goals, we must commit to the learning and with that comes humility.
>
> #ZsZingers #ladyzspeaks #finish

One of my friends and CPA mentors told me early on that the CPA exam had a way of humbling you. This was one of the most accurate statements ever! I didn't come to appreciate it for a while though. I initially thought that once I set aside time to study, it would be easy to FINISH the exam. Unfortunately, this was not the case. I had to commit not only to establishing dedicated study time, but also to learning the material, and really learning myself. The latter part was the hardest.

In a span of 3 months, I got tested for attention deficit disorder (ADD) (because I was convinced this was the reason, I couldn't stay focused on studying), I hired a CPA coach (because I needed help understanding why after 11 years, I could not pass the tests), and I started seeing a therapist (because I needed a person to talk through varying emotions). I remember shedding a tear as I sat in the doctor's office listening to her reading the results of me not having ADD but being pretty quick and sharp. This was obviously a good thing; however, it cleared me of any excuses. It was not that I couldn't focus or retain information; it was that I wouldn't. Ouch! I was not committed to the plan, the process or learning. It was at this point that I knew I had to start from scratch! I could no longer rely on previous learning and study sessions or taking the shortcut to studying. Based on my specific learning style, I had to rebuild a routine. More on this in chapter 5, but long story short, I could no longer rely on my natural abilities and high functioning personality. Humility allowed, and forced, me to approach this journey with fresh eyes and a renewed perspective.

FINISH! *Commit*

> **ZeNai** @LadyZSpeaks
> Sometimes going back to the basics is the only way to FINISH! Be humble
>
> #ZsZingers #ladyzspeaks #finish

FINISH! *Commit*

Writing Prompt:

Document your SMART goals and related objectives

_____

_____

_____

_____

_____

_____

_____

_____

_____

_____

_____

_____

FINISH! *Commit*

Writing Prompt:

Outline the process to achieve your goals

_____

_____

_____

_____

_____

_____

_____

_____

_____

_____

_____

_____

_____

FINISH!

Chapter 3

Chapter 3 | *Distractions*

In 2015 I received my first score release letter from NASBA; the oversight agency for the CPA exam. I sat in my room alone; I immediately opened the letter, and there it was, a 69. Ugh! I needed a 75 to pass. How could this be? I had worked so hard. I studied every night after work; studied while I was traveling for work. I avoided hanging out with friends and family. I followed the recommended study plan; all of this sacrifice for nothing. I had never worked this hard... just to fail. I was devastated. When my parents got home from work, with my brother and his friend, I was bawling crying. I'm pretty sure no one in my family had seen me cry before. I was embarrassed about failing, then embarrassed about crying. I was a mess. My parents did their best to console and reassure me, but it was hard for me to recover.

For a while after, I didn't take the exam seriously. I mean, why would I? I remember going to work and several other people in my start class *had not passed their first part either. Some did, which I was severely annoyed and envious of. But in reality, this was in line with the national passing percentages. Remember, less than or around 50% of people pass various parts of the CPA. It's literally an exam that is not set up for people to pass, in my opinion. At this point in my life, I was no longer willing to sacrifice living my best life to obtain this license. I did however, act like I was getting back on the horse. I applied for different sections; studied here and there, but I could not shake that feeling of failure and embarrassment. I could not focus because I had convinced myself that this was a set up and unattainable. I was less committed to creating boundaries for studying. If I was going to pass, God was going to have to shut things down in my life so I wouldn't have a choice but to focus.*

Well, in 2020, that's exactly what happened. The Covid-19 virus plagued the world and life as usual was no longer. I went from traveling more than 10 times a year for conferences, board meetings, work, and vacation, to zero travel. I went from 3-4 nights of community and church meetings, which would take up a 4-hour block of time, to just 1-2 hours zoom call a of couple nights a week. I went from a 5 to 6-hour chunks of time dedicated to Sunday school and church on Sundays, to a 1.5 hours virtual service. I am not selfish enough to believe that God caused the Pandemic to shut down the world just so I could complete the CPA exam. But I do believe that God makes everything work together for good (Romans 8:28). It was now up to me to take advantage of this newfound free time; free from all the things that kept me distracted from accomplishing this one lingering goal.

The Law of Distraction

Distractions refer to anything that grabs your attention and prevents you from focusing on something else. Distraction is not a positive or negative word; it is simply a realistic acknowledgement of divided attention. According to me, the law of distraction simply means that as soon as you settle on a goal, there will invariably be something that comes up to throw you off track. Every year during the religious season of fasting, amongst other things, my husband and I give up carbs and sweets. It never fails that after making this commitment, co-workers bring in donuts and bagels to work. Not typically one to pass up on free food, I have to practice extreme discipline to not give in to such delicious treats.

Occurrences like this happen in our lives over and over, often as a test to determine your level of commitment. Once we commit to attend church weekly, now all of a sudden there are social events on Sunday. Once we commit to saving money, now every store has a sale. Once we commit to going back to school or obtaining an advanced certification, now we have to increase our hours at work. Once we commit to focus on self-care, here comes a relationship and we spend very little or no time on ourselves. (Insert your own example here.)

The process of removing distractions and taking an inventory of boundaries is not an easy one, but we must be realistic. Distractions will come in the form of opportunities and even selfish ambition, but they only seek to throw you off track and halt your ultimate destiny. Because these aspects of our lives may not be inherently bad, it's often very difficult to identify the necessary separation. During my CPA journey and even my athletic career, there were some things I could not do, places I couldn't go, and people I couldn't interact with.

This is where the phrase "short term sacrifice, bring long term gain" comes in. We must understand that this separation process is short term, and setting boundaries to prevent and overcome distractions increases the chances of completing the goal. If you can be proactive about setting boundaries and focusing on your goals, you will be less reactionary and less likely to be pulled off track. In order to get to where you need to go, separation is necessary! Do not be afraid to move on and forward in the purpose for which God has given you, even if that means cutting some stuff out for a season!

> **ZeNai** @LadyZSpeaks
> As we aim to focus on achieving our goals, we must take an inventory of our current environment, distractions and boundaries that exist, or are missing.
>
> #ZsZinger #ladyzspeaks #finish

Shift Focus

I went into this CPA experience having the best intentions to focus, remove distractions, pass on the first tries, and move on with my life. After being discouraged and eventually not as committed, I allowed myself to be subjected to a mirage of distractions. My focus had definitely shifted from studying for the exam to other priorities that could give me a quick win; I believe this is human nature. When it comes to completing a task on our ever-growing task list, we tend to start with the task that we are most interested in or the task that can be completed quickly. Both of these result in the feeling of immediate gratification. This also allows us to subtly perpetuate the aspect of procrastination, as we continue to put off tackling what's the most important, and usually most difficult, on our list. This process of prioritizing may not seem significant in our daily lives, as many items on our task list do not have hard deadlines; however, the ability to exercise this skill will present itself in other ways.

I had to train myself to tackle the hard thing first. Literally, the first thing I did every morning for almost a year was study. Before the world was awake; I dedicated the first 3 hours of every day to my biggest goal. Before the demands of life started pulling me: when I was able to focus. Before I started thinking about work, working out, checking emails or anything else: I studied. I even set up a

FINISH! *Distractions*

Focus Mode on my Samsung (android) phone. This mode locked all apps except the calculator and camera (for selfie purposes). Having my phone automatically go into Focus Mode helped me stay focused, even when my mind would wander a little bit. If I grabbed my phone out of habit to scroll on social media or check emails, I was literally unable to do so. So instead of going down the social media rabbit hole for 30 minutes, I would get up, stretch, maybe reup on my coffee, take a bathroom break, and get right back to studying. This allowed me to maximize my 3-hour study window. Sometimes we have to create barriers of entry for our lives, not only to remove distractions, but also to shift our focus back to the goal at hand!

Majority of people you will meet tell you that in order to reach your goal, you need to completely cut off the rest of the world, depriving yourself of activities and practices that you need for self-care. To me, this is never a healthy or realistic boundary. Setting aside my daily 3-hour study block of undivided time helped me maintain balance in my life. This is a practice called, Block Scheduling. Mostly used in Corporate America, Block Scheduling involves restricting a dedicated number of hours on your calendar for a specific task. You may see those with heavy calendars block their calendar to have time to perform actual work, take personal calls or simply eat lunch. Blocking out study time for me was crucial, but so was blocking out time to work out, time to go on dates with my husbands, for meetings and church, and yes, time to even work my day job. I was still fulfilled in my personal life and career, while knowing that I was also focused on reaching my goals.

F.O.M.O

Fear of Missing Out (FOMO) refers to the feeling that a person is missing out on something of interest; the feeling of watching others engaged in activities that could be a lot of fun. FOMO is a feeling that can keep us from reaching our potential. For an immediately gratifying experience, we sometimes put our own goals on hold and throw our discipline and focus out of the window. FOMO is one of the most common reasons students give for not wanting to participate in team sports or other school activities. Being an athlete requires setting aside several hours every day to practice and often giving up Friday nights and weekends because of games and tournaments. Committing to sports does cause you to miss out on certain life activities where it seems others are having a good time. As an athlete I missed out on vacations, birthday celebrations, funerals, weddings, baby showers, and hanging out with friends. When it comes to FOMO, I accepted the fact that in order to be the best athlete I could be, there were sacrifices I needed to make and be okay with.

FINISH! *Distractions*

> **ZeNai** @LadyZSpeaks
> As we are seeking to accomplish our goals, we cannot allow ourselves to be distracted by FOMO.
>
> #ZsZingers #ladyzspeaks #finish

Social media also perpetuates the feeling of FOMO. The more access we have to view other people's lives, the more we begin to compare our lives to those that we see online. In multiple studies, social media has been linked to increases in depression, especially in young people under the age of 30. What people post on social media is typically the highlight reel of their life. People tend to share more of the good, than bad. They tend to share the successes, not the failures. This creates a false sense of perfection or a need to be perfect or compete with others. It causes persons to feel like they will never measure up. FOMO will make you think that everyone is living their best life all the time; not considering the challenges or sacrifices that people do not post or share publicly.

This trend was honestly one of the drivers for me documenting my journey in this book. I did not want to paint a picture of perfection, but to discuss the realities of goal achievement. To discuss the necessary sacrifices and provide tips and tools to FINISH! I believe that if we are transparent about our journeys, we can encourage others. I believe that being transparent counteracts the feeling of FOMO because people will understand that all of us have something to overcome. We all have to sacrifice. We all have to create boundaries. In order to reach our best lives, we have to make shorter-term sacrifices, and it is okay.

Even though I wasn't affected by FOMO as an athlete, I was affected when it came to studying for the CPA exam and obtaining the license. In addition to losing motivation and feeling discouraged, FOMO made me feel like others were enjoying the greatest life experiences while I was here studying, which is not a great life experience. The reality is, I really love sports and being an

FINISH! *Distractions*

athlete. I enjoyed the competition and games as well as the process of watching film, practices, learning from coaches and my teammates, traveling, and winning. This is why FOMO didn't affect my athletic career because I was enjoying great life experiences along the way. I had to learn to apply this to my CPA journey. I had to learn to love the studying process! My FOMO moved from the fear of missing out on what others seemed to be experiencing, to the fear of missing out on my own goals and success! At the end of the day, we often place value on things that don't matter because we get immediate pleasure. Take time to value what really matters.

> **ZeNai** @LadyZSpeaks
> Let your FOMO become the fear of missing out on your goals and not what others are doing.
>
> #ZsZingers #ladyzspeaks #finish

Making this mental transition, to release the feeling of FOMO and embrace the realities of sacrifice is not easy. It truly involves self-awareness, determining true intent and creating boundaries. You have to go through the mental exercise of determining what is important right now and what is not. What do need to experience right now and what do you not need? We have to get comfortable with delaying gratification, especially for things that are not in direct alignment with our goals. Zing!

Fun Fact: I am a foodie. People rarely believe me because I am into fitness, having a healthy looking and feeling body. I do also really love food though. All foods, I do not discriminate. My husband and I have our favorite restaurants and eat out several times a week, looking for new places and things to try. I even enjoy fast food, a lot; especially McDonalds and Taco Bell. (Don't care if you judge me either) I follow a lot of food pages on social media and even consistently watch the food network. The way I stay fit is by not overindulging in food all the time. It's about balance. I do not have to eat all of this delicious food all the time. Food is literally not going anywhere so I do not need to indulge every day. During the week, I eat pretty clean and enough for energy and to meet my fitness goals. And then, during social outings and weekends, I allow opportunity to enjoy a bit more. I have created a system of balances that keeps me in line for my personal health goals but also allows for enjoying burgers and fries and bourbon.

We can apply this same thought process to life's other experiences. Instead of feeling the need to indulge and participate all the time, we have to understand that some things we think we are missing out on are actually recurring events. Therefore, we are not missing out on them. The truth is there are very few events that would be considered "a once in a lifetime situation". Having the opportunity to attend the inauguration of the first Black President, once in a lifetime. Taking a trip to Aruba with girlfriends, recurring. Attending your kid's graduation, once in a lifetime. Attending the backyard BBQ for the 4th of July, recurring. These events are subjective and vary by person, but we must individually determine where the lines are. Determine what you can temporarily miss out on. Then stick with it until you have accomplished your goal!

> **ZeNai** @LadyZSpeaks
> You must learn to love the process!
>
> #ZsZingers #ladyzspeaks #finish

Make time, Not excuses

Another barrier to me completing the CPA exam timely was time, or so I thought. I was involved (and still am) in so many things. I would "jokingly" pray that God would add a couple hours to the day so I could get extra things accomplished and checked off my list. Consequently, my task list became a crutch that I would use as an excuse to why I was not passing the exams. Yikes! Between meetings, conferences, work, family, and the gym, I just didn't have enough time to properly dedicate myself to studying. In hindsight, it sounds silly now, but the long and short of it was I did not have my priorities together. Truth is, being disciplined about my schedule, staying organized, working efficiently and timely was not actually an issue for me. I am the person that people call when they want something done. I am an athlete and auditor. I understand processes, meeting deadlines; I possess all the time management tools for completion. It was simply that I had not effectively prioritized. I made time for what I wanted to do and made excuses for what I didn't want to do. I normally consider myself to be proactive and intentional but continuously making these excuses is a characteristic of a procrastinator.

Prior to the Covid-19 pandemic, I read a couple of books and came to the realization that I was actually doing too much which did not contribute to my personal life's goals. I was busy but not personally productive. I allowed my time to be sucked into helping others, lending my voice and talents to other people's missions and purposes, but not advancing my own. So, my excuses for not having time to study for the CPA exam was actually a crutch and a misconception that I had to come to terms with. These books did not reveal groundbreaking information, but definitely forced me to do some hard self-reflection.

FINISH! *Distractions*

My Inspirations:

These are not direct quotes from the book, but key principles that I gathered and interpreted in my own way.

You do not have to say yes to every opportunity that comes your way. Determine the best opportunity for you. The one that aligns with your goal, your core values and the mark that you want to leave in the world. ~ Inspired by *The Best Yes – by Lysa Terkeurst*

To achieve success, you need to be laser focused. That focus should begin as you get out of bed. And you should get out of bed before everyone else! Work hard and grind, even when you do not want to. ~ Inspired by *Rise and Grind – Daymond John*

Stop holding onto people and things that are no longer serving your purpose. People and things who may be draining your energy and therefore become a distraction for you reaching your own personal goals. ~ Inspired by *Necessary Endings – Henry Cloud*

You need to stop with the self-sabotage. Learn to embrace uncertainty and the feeling of self-doubt. Everyone has it but the most successful people use these feelings as fuel to propel them forward. ~ Inspired by Unfu*k Yourself – Gary John Bishop

Time is up for making excuses and procrastinating on your goals. Remove the opportunity for talking yourself out of action. Replace it with a countdown. 5-4-3-2-1 – Go! ~ Inspired by The 5 Second Rule – Mel Robbins

Now, when I say reading, I mean listening to audio books during my commute to work, at the gym or running, or even while styling my hair. One may argue that reading these books was in fact another distraction that kept me from actually studying. I would agree to a certain extent; there are times when I definitely spent a lot of time planning and researching, trying to find motivation to study, instead of actually studying. If I'm honest, I was also looking for some type of short cut. I needed to understand what I was missing and why what I was doing was not working? There had to be some other explanation…right? No. The main theme that I gathered from my readings was understanding the significance of prioritizing what is important and eliminating what is not important. If you continue to give energy to the wrong activity, you may never reach the one goal that you actually want to achieve. That is exactly what I had been doing.

If we are all honest with ourselves, many of the activities on our calendar, many of the tasks on

FINISH! *Distractions*

our to-do list are not for us. They don't contribute to our well-being. They do not get us closer to achieving our personal and professional goals. They don't increase our spirituality. They probably don't even add value to our lives. We have become worker bees and spend time supporting other people's dreams and goals, instead of focusing on ours. We spend more time helping other people rather than managing ourselves. We put more effort into relationships that don't get reciprocated at all. If we are honest with ourselves, we say, "Yes" to many things simply because it makes us feel valued or because it may look good on a resume.

> **ZeNai** @LadyZSpeaks
> What good is it to be the busiest, the most popular, the most whatever…if you are not truly happy and not reaching your goals?
>
> #ZsZingers #ladyzspeaks #finish

Here's some advice: Stop acting like you want to do all the things and say, "No" to being overworked. Let's do better and acknowledge how stretched we are. Choose today and decide what should you need to let go of? What you need to pull back from? Identify, what is not adding value? Maybe you need a new friend circle? Maybe you need to miss a couple parties or brunches? At the end of the day, you can make time to achieve your goals by removing the excuses and activities that are sucking life from you. You must decide that the only thing that matters is whether or not you obtain your goal(s). (Remember, short-term sacrifice, long-term gain)

Because you are reading this book, I would surmise that you have at least one goal to achieve. To get there, you must be willing to do the work and rid yourself of excuses that are holding you back. Excuses are for those that need them. You do not need them anymore. Excuses are tools of the incompetent, uncommitted, and yes, the lazy. You are not these things, or are you? The more we make excuses for why we cannot do something, the easier it is to keep avoiding it and not get it done. The more we make excuses, the more we show others that we may be interested in a goal but not necessarily committed to the path it takes to completion. Making excuses causes us to remain stagnant. We enter a cycle of repetitive starting and stopping and never FINISHing. This is exactly the cycle I found myself in. I was great at thinking about my goal; setting up a plan to study; finding the right materials; doing everything to make it appear as though I was actually planning to study for the exam. I would get up, sit at my desk and not study, but plan to study. I'd become overwhelmed and distracted. Then it was time for work; I had run out of time for studying.

I created a cycle of procrastination, distraction, frustration, and then excuses, which obviously did not work well. You cannot be committed to both your goals and your excuses! Either you want to be great or you want to only talk about being great. At the end of the day, it's not

FINISH! *Distractions*

the will to FINISH! or the process of goal setting that matters. Whether you have already started towards your goal, or if it is just words written on a paper right now, the fact that you have thought about it means that the goal is important to you. If you are going to FINISH, you must have the will to prepare and the will to actually prioritize your goal. The will to make time to do what's important; to focus on the necessary actions required to FINISH!

God did not answer my prayer in the way I had hoped to change the number of hours in a day and expanding the number of days in a week. What He did was show me how to reprioritize and reclaim my time. In addition to the Pandemic's inherent restrictions, I made the decision to let go of some activities, decline new board and committee opportunities, sleep a little less, and change my workout routine. Once I did these things and implemented them consistently, I was able to better manage the time that I had. And

FINISH! *Distractions*

guess what, I was still fulfilled in life. You have to do what you have to do to FINISH!

> **ZeNai** @LadyZSpeaks
> Not being willing to do the work leaves us stagnant, in a repetitive cycle of disruption.
>
> #ZsZingers #ladyzspeaks #finish

FINISH! *Distractions*

Writing Prompt:

Reflect on any distractions that may be shifting your focus, causing you to make excuses and remain stagnant

_____

_____

_____

_____

_____

_____

_____

_____

_____

_____

FINISH! *Distractions*

Writing Prompt:

Document any boundaries you have in place or those you need to implement

_____

_____

_____

_____

_____

_____

_____

_____

_____

_____

_____

_____

FINISH! *Distractions*

Writing Prompt:

In what ways do you experience FOMO? Be honest..

FINISH!

Chapter 4

Chapter 4 | *Recommit*

In track and field, especially the field events, an athlete only has three initial opportunities to compete before they can qualify for the next round. Most meets, because I was pretty good, I ended up throwing six times: three in the preliminary heat and three in the finals. Sometimes, instead of having six good throws, I would only get four good ones and scratch the other two. I remember there were a couple of times I did not make it to the finals because I had scratched too many times or didn't throw it far enough. Scratching a throw is basically like missing a free throw. This disqualifies that throw, resulting in zero points. A scratch occurs when you throw the shot put (or hammer) out of bounds or when your foot touches the outside of the ring. I would often even scratch on purpose if I didn't want that distance counted; for me it was part of the process. After I would scratch a throw, I would find my coach to figure out what I did wrong or tell them what didn't feel right. Then I would

FINISH!   *Recommit*

recommit to doing better the next time I was in the ring. The next time could be in 5 minutes or the next time could be in a couple of days. Either way, there wasn't much time to dwell on the mishap. I still had to get back in the ring and throw again.

*   I wasn't a stranger to recommitting at all. Before I graduated high school, I had committed to attend Rose-Hulman Institute of Technology in Terre Haute, IN. The goal was to become an engineer and play D3 basketball and volleyball. I later received an offer to attend the University of Louisville in Kentucky to throw shot put and hammer on a D1 track team. It was there that I changed my major to accounting. This was in fact a life altering decision. I had to make a decision to recommit to a different path in life. I had to recommit to a different school, a different sports program, and ultimately a different career path. Changing directions can be scary but in life this is inevitable. Being able to recalibrate and commit to a new direction takes time.*

FINISH! *Recommit*

For me recommitting to the CPA exam process was a combination of getting back in the ring and committing to a life altering decision. Though I had failed a couple of exams, all I had to do was find a coach, figure out what I did wrong, recommit to the process, and get back in the ring. But this was easier said than done. I had failed more times than I had passed. The effect these failures had on me was pretty traumatic. I was stagnated for a very long time. I mentioned before not being used to failing so one can imagine my response was not the best. I choose avoidance and dismal. This reaction was different than my reaction to losing a sports competition. With sports, I had more confidence. With sports, I knew I could practice and work on a specific skill. With sport, I could even scout my opponent, in order to be better prepared. I didn't feel that same confidence, ability to practice or even prepare when it came to the CPA exam. I honestly felt like the CPA exam was a lose situation. I felt like it wasn't set up for one to succeed, I mean, remember, there is only a

FINISH! Recommit

50% pass rate per section. That stat alone was discouraging and deflating for me. It was at this point that I needed the most assistance with recommitting to the CPA journey.

> **ZeNai** @LadyZSpeaks
> Failing doesn't mean it's over, it simply means you need to recommit to the process!
>
> #ZsZingers #ladyzspeaks #finish

Learn from Failing
Newsflash: Failing is okay.

This is not a new concept, but it is unfamiliar and uncomfortable to many of us. Just as I had to recover from a bad throw in shotput, I had to learn to apply this concept along my CPA journey. As a serial athlete, my competition level is higher level than most people. I am incredibly competitive, even when playing random games that my dad comes up with in his backyard for us and my niece and nephews. I always want to win. Period! If I don't think that I can win, if I don't feel like putting in the energy to win or if I don't think I can actually succeed, then I simply will not participate. If I cannot be the best, then I just don't get in the game. One of my favorite quotes from the 2006 movie "*Talladega Nights: The Ballad of Ricky Bobby*" with Will Ferrell is, "If you ain't first, you're last". A message Will Ferrell's movie dad left with him after a school career day gone bad. Later in the movie, the dad acknowledged that this concept didn't really make sense, but I still held onto it. Maybe a good concept to apply to sport competitions, but not necessarily to advancing in my career and other goals.

    I needed to think differently about approaching hard things but the idea that failing is okay was inherently foreign to me. I didn't realize I had actually developed a fear of failure. Even using the word failure seems harsh and is a trauma trigger for me. Failure became a motivator for me to be the best at all things, all the time. Which sounds good, but it also paralyzed me on things that I was not inherently good at or interested in.

FINISH! *Recommit*

After hiring a CPA coach to get me through the Exam, she was able to not only help me to shift the way I approached the exam, but she also helped me recover from the failed attempts. We should understand that sometimes failing is a necessary part of the process. It helps us to understand where our weaknesses are and identify areas that need improvement. This is the concept of *failing forward.* Where we accept that failing is not really failing if you learn from the experience. Failure does not make you a failure if you learn from the set back.

> **ZeNai** @LadyZSpeaks
> You are not a failure. If we think about failing simply as not being good at something, the learning opportunities are greater, and the missteps are easier to digest.
>
> #ZsZingers #ladyzspeaks #finish

Recommitting to your process involves an understanding that you may not get everything right the first time but you can always adjust. There may be some additional barriers, whether caused by yourself or external factors. There may be times when you do not FINISH first, or pass, or succeed. Do not let this stop you from moving forward with your plan. Do not let the fear of failure paralyze you from reaching your goals. Do not dwell on your mistakes, shortfalls, and stumbles. Refocus and press on! You may be thinking, this sounds good, but it's easier said than done. And you are correct. It's very easy to write these words on paper. It's very easy to tell someone to just refocus and get back in the game. But be encouraged that I am not speaking in theory, I'm speaking from actual experience.

When I shifted my mindset from feeling like a failure to failing forward, then I was able to succeed. Once I accepted the concept of failing forward, I began to think differently about taking the test; specifically, taking it on test day. Even more importantly was how I would approach the practice test and studying. I started taking the practical application approach instead of listening to hours of lectures and reading. I would review any outline and notes that I had; then spend majority of my study session answering multiple choice questions. Instead of getting discouraged when I didn't get all the practice questions right, I would use the practice questions as additional learning tools. I would review each of the answers I got right to make sure I understood why I got it right and make sure it wasn't a fluke. I would also review all the answers I got wrong and those related explanations. I would also do a deep dive into the concept to make sure I could answer similar questions in the future. For me, the process of studying shifted to quality versus quantity. I was no longer focused on getting through 200 practice questions a day, instead, I just made sure I truly grasps the concepts of the questions I that I was able to get through. This approach worked for me because of my learning style.

FINISH! *Recommit*

> **How to fail forward:**
>
> 1. Remember why you started this process
> 2. Accept that you had a set-back
> 3. Understand that failure does not define who you are
> 4. Analyze your results and determine your weaker areas
> 5. Reassess your study approach and learning style
> 6. Attack your weak areas as if they are new
> 7. Remember why you started this process
> 8. Try again

FINISH! *Recommit*

Ask for Help

Newsflash*:* It's okay to ask for help!

Another concept that is not new; however, it is rarely used because it is uncomfortable. There is a perceived stigma that comes with asking for help. The stigma attached assumes that anyone who asks for help is weak, lazy or not intelligent. It's quite the opposite though. Admitting that you could use and need assistance is a sign of maturity. Even the Bible says, *"If anyone needs wisdom, ask for it"*(James 1:5). The issue is that societal norms cause us to think that everyone that is successful is self-made.

As we talk to other people, watch people on social media, listen to the news and reality TV, what appears to be hard work adds pressure and a false sense of autonomy. Society has glamorized the expectation that people should be overworked. It sounds silly to say, but we see more posts about people being up before the sun and then up all night. We see people getting more certifications;

graduating with more degrees; working multiple jobs and volunteering their time on several boards. It seems like everyone is making life work on their own and you don't see many people posting about the value of mentorship, coaching, networking, counseling, and tutoring. The result: we fall into the comparison trap with false expectations of the journey. We think that everyone is moving forward independently, not knowing the truth or having an understanding of the work that goes on along the way.

People don't always talk about or show the grind along with the community and networks that aid in being successful, which is another part of why I am writing this book. It is important that we are more open and transparent about what it takes to be successful. We must be willing to share not only the highlights and the easy journey, but also what happens when the road gets a little rough. Like my Pastor Husband always says, "Your trials and troubles may be personal, but they are not private."

> **ZeNai** @LadyZSpeaks
> We should normalize sharing tips and best practices that we have learned along the way, including times when we have asked for help.
>
> #ZsZingers #ladyzspeaks #finish

One thing many people can probably agree on is that college does not necessarily prepare you to perform specific job functions. As many accounting classes I had in college; including Audit, when I obtained my first internship at a public accounting firm to conduct audits of public companies, it was a new skill. It was something that I hadn't done before. It required specific training. Onboarding in public accounting, especially for new hires, includes pretty intensive job training. I remember traveling to Chicago for a week before both my internship and full-time jobs began with the same company. I actually enjoyed working for the larger CPA firms because of the travel for clients and the training experience. It allowed me to meet people from the organization around the country and it was a great learning environment.

For new hires, the first year's training included an overview of the firm and specific direction of the audit process. It covered everything from planning the engagement to audit procedures for each financial statement account to various accounting and audit compliance regulations and much more. Depending on the size of the public accounting firm, this training would occur every year or couple of years. One thing the trainers, who were fellow auditors in the firm, would repeat over and over was "This is a lot of information and you will not remember it all. Do not hesitate to ask questions."

Another popular training quote was "Do not spin your wheels". The point of these directives was for us to not waste time thinking that we had to figure out the answers on our own. As a staff, it is completely inefficient to stare at the computer for 8 hours, trying to figure out why certain numbers do not agree with what the client provided or to try to figure out what step is next in the audit. The goal of an audit is to get the job done effectively and efficiently. Basically, the audit is to be done correctly in the hours that have been budgeted for the work. This allowed us to charge the client what was quoted for the job. Spinning your wheels is not efficient. Asking another auditor on the team for guidance not only saved time on the audit engagement, but it also helps the new auditor to learn quicker and makes sure they are moving in the right direction. Reflecting on my beginning process and approach as a young auditor helped me to remember the power of asking for help.

    Definitely the turning point for me passing the exam was asking for help, which meant hiring a CPA coach. In all of my research on how to pass the exam, looking for short-cuts and fool proof strategy, I came across several ads for CPA coaches and mentors. I watched hours of YouTube videos and followed a lot of CPA personalities on Instagram. I had basically gone down a rabbit hole and the internet algorithms were throwing me CPA courses and people left and right. I had signed up for a couple newsletters and webinars but I am still not sure how I ended up on a phone call with Erin Daiber with Well-Balanced Accountants. Probably a nudge by the Holy Spirit, in addition to me appreciating the word balanced in her company name. Long story short, I was sold on her approach, she was super relatable and I felt like she understood the journey I had been on. We agreed that I didn't need her to teach me accounting concepts, but I needed her to help me create a structure to pass, which included learning about myself. I paid around two thousand dollars over 4 months to learn how to pass the exam. I initially felt like this was a last-ditch effort, but ultimately asking for help was a lifesaver. (Remember earlier, I mentioned how much time and energy I had put into this exam, with little success.)

Over 11 years, I had invested thousands of dollars. After spending 4 months with my CPA

FINISH!   *Recommit*

coach, I ended up passing all four parts of the exam in seven months (FAR 8/25/2021, BEC 9/15/2021, AUD 11/10/2021, and REG 2/23/2022). What prolonged for 12 years because I didn't ask for the proper help, took me only seven months to complete. Whatever your goal is, whether it is to obtain a professional certification or additional degree, start a new business, or save up to buy a house; do not be afraid to ask questions. Do not waste time spinning your wheels trying to figure out what you do not know. I am not saying you have to spend thousands of dollars to get help, but you should definitely make a commitment to seeking guidance.

> **ZeNai** @LadyZSpeaks
> Asking for help allows us to be more efficient and can keep us moving in the right direction. Don't be afraid to do so!
>
> #ZsZingers #ladyzspeaks #finish

FINISH! *Recommit*

Give Yourself Grace

Whether we do it subconsciously or not; whether we want to admit it or not, we compare ourselves, accomplishments, and our life to others. Especially in this age of social media, we subconsciously internalize what other people are doing and how they look. We then use that as a benchmark to judge our own lives. When we do this, compare our lives, judge our lives, and it can cause us to rush into something we are not ready for, and ultimately move outside of purpose. We tend to be our own hardest critics. This causes us to not appreciate the good things about ourself and our life. We become overly critical of our faults and failures. But like the famous rapper Cardi B alludes to in her song, "Best Life", *we must stop competing with other people and start competing with ourselves.* To me, this means, giving myself grace.

Grace, according to the Bible is defined as unmerited favor given to us from God. God loves us so much that despite our shortcomings, He still looks after us, cares for us, and provides help to us. (Do not be alarmed that I mentioned God and Cardi B in the same breath; it's called balance.) And the point is, that we should not compare ourselves to where other people are in their journey but instead offer ourselves the same grace that God gives us. Not because we are perfect, but because we love ourselves enough to keep pressing forward. Offering ourselves grace, forgiving ourselves, and letting go of past faults and failures are all actions that should be practiced daily. This CPA journey taught me how to remove the veil of guilt, shame, and discouragement and to shift to appreciating my journey.

Even though I am naturally shy, I have never had a problem with confidence. However, I did have to get comfortable with allowing myself to acknowledge the good and not dwell on the bad. In 2017, I was selected by Junior Achievement of Indianapolis as one of the Best and Brightest, top 10 upcoming leaders in the accounting and finance profession. As I was talking to my parents about it,

I admitted that I didn't necessarily think I deserved it because I hadn't FINISHed the CPA exam yet; mind you, the CPA license was not a criterion for this award. Now, I know most parents are typically biased cheerleaders that support their kids to the end. My parents are exactly that, but they also are realistic, honest, and they do not have a problem telling it like it is. When I tried to downplay this nomination, my dad said "Whaaaat?!" You would have thought I said bad words to him. Both he and my mom proceeded to remind me how hard I worked in my career, how they admired my commitment to the community and volunteering and in general, how awesome I was. After about 7 minutes of this encouragement, behind a couple silent tears, I accepted their perspective. They were 100% right. I did deserve this recognition for my contributions to the accounting profession. I did deserve to win (which I didn't but I'll save my thoughts on that for another time). My not reaching one goal should not and did not negate the other

FINISH! *Recommit*

successes that I had achieved. I needed to acknowledge that... and so do you.

What I also came to realize is that I was sabotaging myself. Not an easy conclusion to come to. As goal-oriented achievers, we must get comfortable at acknowledging our limitations. Understanding that getting yourself together requires a level of honesty and humility that may be unfamiliar. There is nothing easy about realizing that you're the one who's been holding yourself back. That maybe your lack of discipline is the answer to why you have not FINISHed what you started. I know specifically for me, as a black woman, an athlete, a type A, OCD personality, I tend to take on everything. My enneagram type is also type 3, Achiever, which describes my personality as self-assured and ambitious but also status conscious and highly driven. All that said, I used to believe that if I wanted something done and done right, I needed to do it myself. This is a very limiting and controlling belief system. It is not a good perspective as a leader whose responsibility is to develop others. Trying to take on everything, and do everything, and be everything for everyone, for me, was a form of self-sabotage.

Psychology Today describes self-sabotage as behavior that "creates problems in daily life and interferes with long-standing goals." Whether we actively or passively do it, we have to be careful of behaviors, thoughts and actions that are contrary to our end goals. Things that we do to ourselves. Things that we have to take responsibility for. Things that we allow to get us off track. We must be mindful of these behaviors so we can recognize the danger and detours they may cause. We must be honest about these behaviors so we can correct them and move forward.

The reality is that we cannot do it all on our own. Believing that we can and should causes us to take on more than we should. This leads to burn out, frustration, and mistakes. In my case, trying to take on so much, not asking for help prolonged my achieving my goals. Truth is I was not able to do everything and I needed to be okay with this. So do you. Giving yourself grace allows for mistakes. Giving yourself grace allows for patience. Giving yourself self allows for reflection. Giving yourself grace allows for self-love. Giving yourself grace allows you to not beat yourself up and forgive yourself. Giving yourself grace allows you to be free. You can give yourself grace and still be impactful. You can give yourself grace and still be motivated and complete your goals.

Giving yourself grace is not an excuse to accept mediocrity or failure. It is simply an acknowledgment that things can happen. Understand that your outcome will be determined by how you respond to your challenges and so called "failures". When you do not give yourself grace, but instead choose to beat yourself up, it will cause you to eventually give up all together.

FINISH! *Recommit*

> **ZeNai** @LadyZSpeaks
> Love yourself enough to understand that while your path may not be perfect, you are still good enough to FINISH! Give yourself #grace!
>
> #ZsZingers #ladyzspeaks #finish

FINISH! *Recommit*

Writing Prompt:

What have you learned along the journey?

_____
_____
_____
_____
_____
_____
_____
_____
_____
_____
_____
_____
_____

FINISH! *Recommit*

Writing Prompt:

Outline your recommitment plan

_____

_____

_____

_____

_____

_____

_____

_____

_____

_____

_____

_____

FINISH! *Recommit*

Writing Prompt:

Where do you need to give yourself grace?

_____

_____

_____

_____

_____

_____

_____

_____

_____

_____

_____

_____

FINISH!

Chapter 5

Chapter 5 | *FINISH*

Fun Fact: I love my husband, but he was not the best accountability partner, or was he? Maybe he just did not show it in the way I thought I needed. My husband believes that people need to figure things out on their own, versus always being instructed or restricted. I, however, wanted him to be stricter on me. Once he saw that I was serious about this process and once I actually communicated some realistic ways he could help me, I felt like he became more vested in my CPA studying process but still never gave restrictions. There were several times I needed a shoulder to cry on from the weight of studying, failing, questioning life and myself in general. He was actually a great motivational support, and I am grateful for his nurturing and keeping a close eye on my emotional space as I navigated this journey.

My husband himself is actually a very disciplined and motivated man. The way we study, however, and focus is completely different. My husband can be watching TV and studying the Bible or his schoolwork all at the same time and comprehend them all. Not me. My husband can stay up way late to do his work. Not me. Our evenings mostly include watching tv for an hour or two after dinner, meetings etc. We would often do so while also checking emails or prepping for meetings. I like to think of it as productive tv time. The exception, though, was that I could not watch tv and study at the same time. I would often get upset at my husband (I never told him this) because I felt like he wasn't holding me accountable when I said I needed to study or restrict tv. I wanted him to hold me accountable by saying, "No tv today, don't you need to study?"

Newsflash: *this was not my husband's job.*

It was an unfair expectation I put onto him, which he wasn't aware of. What I was actually doing was projecting my own guilt for procrastinating onto my husband. Don't do this. It's not realistic or fair to your spouse. My husband was indeed incredibly supportive in the ways that actually mattered. He could not, however, force me to be motivated or disciplined to study; that was on me. If he did try, I would probably have gotten an attitude, which would also have been counterproductive. After several years of marriage, I'm confident my husband understands my personality, my attitude and the need for me to sometimes figure things out along the way. This has saved us many arguments, but also has helped me reflect internally and grow stronger in the places where I had become reliant on others and outside accountability.

Communicating your goal to others is important and was a vital part of my accountability and study process. It was important for me to communicate to my spouse, my family, and my friends so they could be supportive of my goal. It was not necessary for them to understand the process, but it was important that they understood the intensity and importance. Initially I did not share as much because I did not want people to keep asking how the studying was going. Because I wanted to seem like superwoman and didn't want anyone to make excuses or concessions for me. Also, because I didn't want the embarrassment of sharing if I did not pass, especially after years of being on this journey. When I did begin to share, the burden of secrecy was lifted. I was also able to set clear expectations and boundaries, which was easier for my circle to accept because they understood what my end goal was. I encourage people to be transparent and share their goals for the motivation and also the accountability. Having people check in on you can do one of two things: it can make you feel bad about slacking or it can make you feel supported through the process. If you are truly committed to your goal, hopefully you will feel supported more often than you feel like a slacker. But remember, no one can want something more than you. No one can force you to do anything. If someone does try to force you, your heart and mind won't be committed. No one should want you to achieve your goal more than you. Zing!

The same happens in sports, as much as coaches are there to lead and guide and support us, it's up to the athlete to determine whether they will give 100% at practice. It's up to the athlete to determine whether they will get enough rest and eat right consistently. As awesome as my college coach was, he could not get in the ring and compete or throw for me. As much as he wanted me to win, he could not want me to win more than I wanted it. It was up to me to get in the ring; apply the techniques I had learned and practiced, and FINISH! the throw! It was up to me to independently execute.

This mindset of independent execution ultimately helped me FINISH! the CPA exam. I created a rigorous schedule that allowed me to have uninterrupted study time and keep my other commitments. My schedule was as followed:

FINISH!   *FINISH*

5:15 am	*Wake up*
5:30 - 8:30 am	*Study*
8:30 – 9:00 am	*Shower and Prep for Day*
9:00 – 4:00 pm	*Work*
5:00 - 6:30 pm	*Workout*
7:00 - 8:30 pm	*Dinner, Bible study, Meetings, etc*
9:00 - 10:30 pm	*TV time with review notes or emails*
10:30 – 11:00 pm	*Sleep*
	*Repeat*

On the Saturdays and Sundays, I would study from 6-9am, nap throughout the day and make up any work I let slide during the week.

This schedule looks remarkably similar to the schedule I kept in college. There were sacrifices made during each of these seasons of my life. But like then, if I was going to FINISH! I had to really hone in. I had to be both intentional and committed to the FINISH! and to not losing pieces of myself and neglecting my responsibilities. This approach worked for me. It also worked for my other new CPA friends from my accountability group. While their schedules varied slightly, the

FINISH! *FINISH*

routine and dedication were, had to be and remained consistent to FINISH! And we did exactly that! We FINISHed! A Scripture that I applied to my journey was 2nd Timothy 4:7, "I have fought the good fight, I have FINISHed the race, I have kept the faith."

Start by Starting

Just start. Easier said than done, I know. A mentor and good friend of mine says, *"Starting somewhere is better than not starting anywhere and always better than not starting at all"* (Dr. Tuesday Tate). Whatever you are thinking about doing, make a decision to start moving in that direction. Don't waste another day over thinking, over planning, over explaining. Don't waste another minute second-guessing and questioning. Don't waste another second procrastinating and justifying. Do not wait to be in the mood. Just start. And if you have to start, re-start, start over, do it as many times as necessary. Remember however, no matter how many times you start, the key to achieving your goal is to FINISH!

Having big goals and ideas can be exciting. The thought of accomplishing something you have never done before can be thrilling. Imagining what this accomplishment will mean for your career, your health, your family, your faith, and maybe your community. Strangely, that same exhilarating feeling can launch us right into feeling overwhelmed. Especially if it's something you have tried before, but for whatever reason, you didn't FINISH or didn't succeed at. It may be something you have talked about for years but never taken steps to complete and now you are ready to move forward. Or it could be something you have seen others try and not be successful at and now you have doubt.

I was guilty of letting this feeling of being overwhelmed cause additional confusion, frustration, and procrastination. With such a big goal of obtaining my CPA license, it was difficult for me to digest the enormity of the goal. I knew passing the CPA exam could open more doors for me in my career. I knew FINISHing would be a sigh of relief and weight off my shoulders. Yet still, saying I was going to begin studying on a Monday would give me anxiety. It was like I never felt fully prepared to start and for some reason I could not see the FINISH line. It was like I was not confident in the plan that I had laid out. I remember getting up to study, but instead of studying, I would end up doing more research on the best ways to study and spend time redoing my study schedule and approach.

Remember, I am an extreme planner. I think it's part of my DNA; enhanced by a lifetime of structure: balancing sports, school, and other commitments. Heighten by my career as an auditor, juggling over 20 clients a year with the various deadlines and compliance regulations. One of the core beliefs I try to lean into says "You need a solid plan at the beginning so you can FINISH on time" (see chapter one: planning section). This planning though became my crutch and my excuse. It became a distraction and procrastination tool. It was both a blessing and a curse. One 5am morning a revelation finally hit me: "I need to just start studying, otherwise, I will literally never FINISH!"

Getting back on the horse is never easy. This is why consistency and discipline are preached so much when it comes to fitness. Once you get in the routine, working out becomes part of your normal schedule and your body begins to adjust. Being an athlete, fitness is something that has been ingrained in me for a very long time. With that however; I still feel the pains of getting back in the routine once I have stopped for a little bit. Because I like variety, every couple of months, I switch up the types of workouts I do. The majority of my time is spent weight training, but I also add in running, yoga and various high intensity interval training classes. Running is the hardest.

When training for the Spartan races in 2019, I worked myself up to running 8 miles at a time. It wasn't easy but I could consistently do it. After the racing season was over though, I stopped running as consistently. After a couple months of just weights and treadmill work, I decided to get back to running. After just one mile, I wanted to quit. I ended up having to do two miles that day because I was one mile away from home and had to get back. It was not 8 miles but I was proud of myself, nonetheless. I had made a decision to get up and run. And I did just that. I wasn't going to be able to run 8 miles right away but I had to start somewhere. And that somewhere meant, getting out of bed, walking outside and just starting to run. That first run of the season was a launch day to get me back focused and in the routine. I removed all barriers: didn't have to drive anywhere, set my clothes out the night before, and simply walked outside! From there, I was running (in my best Forest Gump voice)!

FINISH!

FINISH

The key to FINISHing is to start. Even if things are not as buttoned up as you would like them to be; it is important to start somewhere. Start by doing something productive towards the goal. If the goal is to complete a certification, start studying today. If your goal is to go back to school, apply today. If your goal is to start a business, start your business plan today, choose a name and register the business. If the goal is to clean your house, throw away those old papers, wash the dishes, etc., start today. Do not let the need for all things and the outcome to be perfect get in the way of getting started or you progressing.

One thing I have learned over the years is that even when you think you have a solid plan, adjustments will be needed. You may need to make adjustments because of your work schedule, because of your family commitments, your networking and community involvements, and maybe even the change in seasons. You do not have to throw the baby out with the bath water, assuming that if you cannot maintain the same plan and schedule forever your plans won't work. Instead, just allow for some flexibility in your plan. I learned this the hard way, especially during the summertime or when I was traveling a lot for work or meetings. If I could not study the same time every day, or even as commitments snuck on my calendar, I would stop studying completely; instead of adjusting my schedule, I allowed a disruption in my plan to get me off track. Be careful and diligent with this! We should not get caught up in creating a perfect plan, because that does not exist. We should allow for flexibility. Planning itself can become a subtle barrier, a tool for procrastination and ultimately a disruption. Do not allow it!

> **ZeNai** @LadyZSpeaks
> Trust your plan and just get started! Remember, the key to FINISHing is to start!
>
> #ZsZingers #ladyzspeaks #finish

Establish Purposeful Boundaries

Activity without purpose is the drain of your life. I'm not sure who said this, but it's another concept that we all need to embrace. We are living in a time where it's easy to be pulled in many different directions. It is important to ensure the activities we are participating in align with our goals and objectives. We all want to live our best lives, brunch with friends, travel the world, gain more and have more. We have to be careful to not to be distracted from the immediate necessary grind. During this CPA journey, I learned to be okay with missing out on some things and some people. I learned that the grind was necessary but only temporary. Because of my foundational structure and internal boundaries that I was very good at creating, I was eventually able to create a CPA bubble where I could be laser focused. No matter how much I shared my goals openly, there would always be the pull and attraction of doing something a little more exciting with people that I actually enjoyed. I literally had to put a hold on parts of my social life, and with the help of the Covid-19 pandemic, I was able to maintain many of my relationships. Well, at least ones that I cared about. The Pandemic became my way of escape, my (all of our) legitimate reason to stay home. This allowed me more time to study.

> **NOTE;** *You may be thinking that I was lucky the pandemic came. That the pandemic was the only reason I accomplished my goals. You would be partially correct in that assessment but must also take into account this one principle: opportunities may present themselves, but you have to be disciplined enough to take advantage of them. During the pandemic of 2020, we saw an increase in depression, suicides, divorce, unproductiveness and even brain fog. Some people were solely focused on surviving the pandemic, and that is okay. Something inside of me could not miss this moment though. I could not let any more time be*

wasted. I had been surviving long enough, it was time to thrive!

The reality is, everyone won't understand your journey, your level of commitment. And that's okay because it's not for them to. Everyone will not understand or respect your boundaries. This is why it is so imperative for you to show your respect for the goals established. Everyone will not understand your purpose, because it wasn't given to them. It was given to you. So be careful whom you surround yourself with. Make sure they are people who support you, your vision, your purpose, and once you have told them the process; make sure they are in it to win it with you. An added plus is being able to surround yourself with people who have had similar experiences.

> **ZeNai** @LadyZSpeaks
> Your actions must line up with your goals if you are going to achieve success!
>
> #ZsZingers #ladyzspeaks #finish

I've always been a huge supporter of accountability and teamwork. It probably stems from being an athlete for the greater part of my life. Of all the sports I played, I like to think that being a thrower in track and field is one of the best examples (hence the premise of this book and the shot put I'm holding on the cover). Most people do not think of track as a team sport but it does have aspects of such. I describe track and field as an individual team sport. As a thrower, I competed individually in the shot put and hammer; with the goal of having the furthest throw. If I threw the furthest, FINISHing in first place, then I would get ten points. If I FINISHed first place in both events, I could earn twenty points. Twenty points would then be added to the overall team score to determine a winner of the meet.

The individual aspect was great because I was in complete control of my individual outcome. In addition, even if my team did not win the meet, the distance of my throw would be what determined whether or not I qualified for regional or national level tournaments, which I did multiple times. Compared to basketball or volleyball where regardless of your individual performance, your team has to win in order for you as a member of the team to move to the next level. While competing to be the best individually, it was great to have other throwers around, my teammates who were doing the same thing. We practiced together. Traveled together. Lived together. Ate together. For 5 years, my college teammates and I did life together. Yet, at the end of the day, we were competing to throw the farthest and make it to nationals on the individual level. I literally took this concept and recreated this experience to help me pass the CPA exam.

In March 2020, I posted a question in the discussion board of the National Association of Black Accountants (NABA), where I am the Central Region President and a National Director: "Anyone interested in having virtual study sessions? Could use some accountability partners during this

COVID-19 lockdown. We could use zoom meetings and watch each other study." The discussion board lit up. Initially there were about 25 people on the zoom discussion call. A year later, we have over 380 people in the community study group. It is now called the NABA CPA Bound program (www.nabainc.org/cpabound). It is a community where NABA members can join for study accountability and encouragement as well as for resources, mentorship and potential connection for jobs and scholarships.

Here is the interesting part, this is not a guided program where someone is teaching CPA material. It is a group of like-minded, mostly business professionals who have been struggling to complete the CPA exam. The group has expanded to include graduate students and others who are new to the profession, but the foundation was built by people like myself. People who are mid-career and needed a circle of friends who understand the journey. It is a community of self-motivated, high driven people who just need a little accountability and community of people with the same goals to move through the study process. When I said I was waking up at 5 am to study in the mornings, there were always 3-5 other people on Zoom studying independently. When I said I was studying on the weekends, there were always other people on Zoom studying. As I got closer to sitting for my last section of the exam, me and another girl (Robyn) from Maryland became partners. We would hop on zoom together, sometimes twice a day, go through questions, share tips and other notes. It reminded me of my senior year in track when only a couple other teammates and I qualified for Nationals. It wasn't the whole team, just us focused on the FINISH line. Same with Robyn. We studied in the mornings together. We met in the evenings sometimes. We even took the test within a week of each other. We also found out (together) we passed the last part, Regulation (tax section) on the same day. Having people like Robyn, Carmen, Niles, Shacquerra, Elizabeth, Mourghan, Sarah, and many others to study with and lean on was another major key! They understood what I was going through, striving to achieve and they understood the process. They could appreciate the high and lows of the journey. They understood the necessary boundaries. We were in each other's bubble and were able to and did FINISH! together.

You may not be an athlete or be able to create an accountability community like I did, but you can create boundaries and you can establish a bubble. Anything and anyone that doesn't align with you FINISHing what you have started should be put aside and replaced with actions and people that will help you reach the FINISH line.

ZeNai @LadyZSpeaks
You have to stay committed to the process, even if it only makes sense to you!

#ZsZingers #ladyzspeaks #finish

FINISH!

Say this with me: *I owe it to myself to FINISH!*

You have to believe this. You have to show up for yourself. I wanted to give up on this goal so many times but 2020 was a turning point for me and the CPA license. The problem was, even though I wanted to throw in the towel, I had already invested so much time and energy (and money). Even with the "failures" and lack of motivation, I was not willing to let all of that go to waste. I definitely do not believe in wasting time or money and, honestly, that has been the most frustrating part of this whole journey.

More than almost anything intangible, I value my time. I believe that if you are not 15 minutes early, you are late. This probably stems from having to be ready for practice to start right on the nose. There was no walking in when practice was supposed to start, you needed to be dressed and semi warmed up. I also believe that if you spend time or energy on something, you should have something to show for it. Even now, I hate attending meetings and leaving with no action items. So, imagine being on this CPA journey for 12 years and having nothing to show for it. This ate me from the inside out like nobody's business. I'm pretty confident it's the sole reason that I have some many gray hairs right now. But I still could not quit. I couldn't quit because it meant that my career options would be limited. But more importantly, quitting meant that I had wasted time and money. Quitting would mean that I gave up on myself. Quitting meant that I was a hypocrite. How could I preach accountability, discipline, and focus, but not be able to apply it myself? I could not let that narrative live anymore. Nope. And neither should you.

Keep in your mind *why* you started! Whatever your goal is and whatever you need to do, to keep that thought of "why" in front of you; you gotta do it. I had to physically write the goal down on my electronic vision board. I printed it out and put it in front of the mirror where I brush my

FINISH!   *FINISH*

teeth every morning. I also wrote my goals down on the mirror in my bathroom and on a post-it and put it on my computer screen. Study times were on my calendar and a lot of my social media posts were about the exam. When I tell you I was tapped in and became laser focused, I was and I did.

    My friend, remember why you started down this journey. Remember the initial excitement and keep that same energy! We typically start off strong then get distracted or detoured by life's twist and turns. Do not worry about any obstacles! No matter how long or how far you have fallen off, you can get back on the horse! Do not let your time, money or dream go to waste!

ZeNai @LadyZSpeaks
Remember why you started and leverage that energy and momentum!

#ZsZingers #ladyzspeaks #finish

FINISH! *FINISH*

Writing Prompt:

What is keeping you from just starting?

_____
_____
_____
_____
_____
_____
_____
_____
_____
_____
_____

FINISH! *FINISH*

Writing Prompt:

How can you establish better boundaries and a circle of accountability?

_____

_____

_____

_____

_____

_____

_____

_____

_____

_____

_____

FINISH!

CONCLUSION

CONCLUSION

The day I received notice I passed the last part of the CPA exam was arguably the best day of my life. I mean, it's right up there with winning the Marion County Volleyball tournament in high school, the Big East Championship in college and, of course, marrying my husband. Those are all vivid memories. Realizing that I was finally done with the CPA exam though was so surreal. Honestly, I expected to win tournaments; I expected to get married; yet, I still struggled with feeling confident with the CPA exam. Even until the last test, the Regulation section (i.e., tax) which I had taken three times before between November 2020 and January 2021. When I received the alert that testing scores had been released, I remember sitting on the couch with my husband; a man of great faith. I asked my him if we should look or if we should wait.

When I first started taking these exams, I was so nervous I would not say anything about score release day. I would wait a day or sometimes even a week to see the results, especially before scores were available online and when they would be mailed or emailed to you. I would let the notification sit there until I was indifferent. Crazy, I know. But after I started the CPA Bound community, my confidence began to grow, along with my anticipation. My other candidate friends would post in the group when they checked their score. Some people would pass and the chat would go crazy with congratulation messages. Some people would not pass and the chat would go crazy with encouraging messages to stick with it. Regardless of the outcome, it was a motivating experience and felt good to be surrounded (virtually) with people on the same roller coaster.

So, on February 24, 2021, my husband made me rip the band aid off. This was it! I logged into the portal and saw a 79! I wanted to pass out. I was in disbelief! Was this really it?!? Had I really passed the last section, finally?! A passing score for the CPA exam is a 75. I asked my husband at least 3 times to double check. "What do I need to pass?" He said, "75, I think!" "What does this say" He said "79!" "So, I'm done?" He said "Yes!!!"

Such a great day! It was probably 9pm at this point. I called my family on the House Party app; my parents were already in bed but they knew to answer because I very rarely call on the phone. Next, I called my 3 BFFs. All my people knew to answer the phone. They thought one of two things: either "Z is pregnant or she is done with the exam". My girlfriend in Atlanta was already in the kitchen with a bottle of wine ready to crack open. My other friend in Bloomington was already having margaritas. My husband came through with some celebratory Jack Daniel's shots! It was great! I didn't cry then...but I felt like I probably should have.

So, while I did not have a physical baby that day, something was definitely born. A new CPA entered the world.... one that had been baking for 12 long years. One that had experienced heartache, disappointment, embarrassment but

FINISH! *CONCLUSION*

now joy and relief! One that was ready to walk in purpose and change the world! A new black girl CPA who preserved until the end! Me!!

<u>Call to Action</u>

Congratulations on FINISHING this book! Now what goal have you put on the shelf, never to see light again? It is time to go grab it. Consider this your first step towards the completion of that goal. Over the course of this book, you have documented your thoughts, your goals, your pain points and more. The next couple pages serve as reminders to help you pull nuggets from the book without having to read again. I do recommend, however, reading this and your notes multiple times. Leave this book and your notes on your desk or working space as a motivational tool! Even though this is my personal journey, continuously reading and incorporating your thoughts will serve as a reminder to keep pressing forward in purpose! I do not want you to simply know my journey, I want you to learn from my experiences and apply them

FINISH! *CONCLUSION*

for your success! Foot on the gas! Full steam ahead. I want to experience the same relief I have!

Today is your day to change your mindset and make a decision to succeed, no matter what. We often get discouraged and get thrown off track when we expect things to go smoothly, and they don't. When we do not expect obstacles to get in the way, we will find ourselves side-swiped by them. Remember my Spartan Race experiences? If I showed up to run a mini marathon, which is straight-up running, I would be very upset if there were obstacles on the route. I would be unprepared if all of a sudden there were a wall to climb, mudslides, and a sandbag to carry. With the Spartan Races, we expect there to be obstacles. The obstacles are actually published in advance so you can practice getting over and through them. While you may not be able to prepare for the ups and downs of life, knowing the potential of their existence makes the process a bit more manageable. Trust me! Work hard! Be committed.

FINISH! *CONCLUSION*

And never, under any circumstances, should you give up!

One of my favorite Bible teachers, Joyce Meyer, wrote a book and has a sermon series entitled: "Battlefield of the Mind". Without reading the book, you can understand the premise. Whether you are able to win the battle or in this case, achieve your goal, the victory - the win is determined in your mind. It's based with what you believe, how you talk to yourself, how to communicate your goal and how you understand the process. Your success is based on your ability to envision your success. If you cannot see it right away, however, if you still have questions, I say, "Fake it until you make it!" This has been a mantra of mine for a long time. I often admit to people that I am a naturally shy person; they rarely believe me though because I've gotten good at owning the space and opportunities, I find myself in. Growing up I did not necessarily want the spotlight and additional attention, but I was always pulled into leadership. I was made captain of all my sports teams, I was always the group leader in class, I was an officer for my graduating class. Literally, I was always the leader so I gained the ability at an early age to fake confidence until I actually had it. I became more fearful of failing in front of people than speaking in front of people. For a long time, I would fake like I felt comfortable leading. It wasn't until recently that I realized I wasn't faking anymore. I had actually started believing in myself. Now, look, here I am, writing a book and speaking in front audiences with more to come. Why, how? Because I won the battle in my mind. The battle of whether or not I could do anything I put my mind to (Philippians 4:13).

Take things one-step at a time. The decision to FINISH what you have started or plan to begin your journey is black and white; there is no gray area. Either you will do it or you won't. Either you believe you can or you don't. Once you have made the decision to FINISH, however, there will be gray space. Don't let the gray areas of confusion;

FINISH! CONCLUSION

indecision, and uncertainty stop you. Win the battle in your mind!

> *You can be disciplined.*
> *You can be committed.*
> *You can do this!*
> *You can FINISH!*

And once you do, the feeling of completion will be overwhelmingly rewarding!

Success

To be successful as an accountant, a person does not need to have the CPA license. There are a variety of career paths and opportunities for success without the license. When I worked in Corporate America for a short stint, between Public Accounting firms, I remember talking to some of the accounting leaders (i.e., CFO, VP of Finance, etc.), seeking their advice on obtain the CPA license. Instead of promoting the CPA license, I felt like it was downplayed with little encouragement to attain it. I believe there were only one or two others in the whole accounting and finance team who had their CPA license. Actually, many of my friends in the industry are extremely successful and they are not CPAs, and that is okay. Because everyone's path is different.

Interestingly, while I was waiting to receive my license, I received a job offer to leave public accounting, no longer working at a CPA firm. I still get the question, what was the point of the CPA license if you are not going to work at a firm or start your own business? Well, first of all, the CPA license is also beneficial to those who work in Corporate America, like I do now. It is not just for those in CPA firms (and it is not just for those who do taxes, for the record.) So, let me circle back to the benefits of having the license, as noted by the National Association of State Board of Accountancy (NASBA):

- Prestige and Respect
- Career Development
- Career Security
- Job Satisfaction
- Salary and Benefits

FINISH! *CONCLUSION*

The other reason I wanted to obtain a CPA license is because I said I would!! The added benefit of no longer having this cloud over my head.

Generally, success is typically defined as the accomplishment of an aim or purpose. Society also tends to measure success based on how much money someone has, how nice their clothes are, even certain careers and position. These may be good measures for certain people but can also be deceiving. It is important to not be distracted by the glitz and glam that life has to offer, but be focused on your purpose and goals and the path to get there. By many people's standards, they considered me to be successful. I guess to a certain extent I was. I had a good job. I kept myself in shape. I wore nice clothes. I had a loving supportive husband. I held pretty important positions. But these things did not define success for me. For a very long time, I personally defined success as winning. I am sure this is not surprising to you with my history of athlete achievements.

You can imagine the mental toll the CPA journey had on me, leaving me to not feel as successful, despite the other positive things in my life: remember imposter syndrome. What I had to learn eventually was that success for me, does not only occur at the end, in the winning stage. Success occurs along the journey. Success is the ability to stick to the path of accomplishment. Success for me was met by reaching those little milestones I set for myself in outlining my SMART goals. Many of us struggle to FINISH, and even start, because we are intimidated by seeing the success of others. Once I redefined what success was for me, my confidence began to grow. I became more clear and more comfortable on the path to FINISHing my goals.

So, define what success looks like for you. Write it down and review it consistently. I created a vision board using pictures and quotes I found online. I printed out a picture of my vision board from CVS and put a copy in my personal journal and another framed copy on my bathroom mirror.

FINISH! *CONCLUSION*

This way, I saw success whenever I washed my face and brushed my teeth and even whenever I opened my notebook at a coffee shop. My goals, my ambitions and my dreams were always in front of me, which helped me stay focused and eventually succeed. My childhood pastor, the late Rev. L.A. Manual would also say *"Keep the main thing, the main thing!"* This was my interpretation of that.

FINISH! *CONCLUSION*

Writing Prompt:

What does success look like for you?

_____

_____

_____

_____

_____

_____

_____

_____

_____

_____

_____

FINISH! *CONCLUSION*

Significance

Someone is waiting for you to FINISH! Whether said person is you, a sibling, a mentee or someone you do not know, your actions (or lack thereof) have influencing potential. You have an opportunity to have a larger cultural and community impact. No pressure right! But consider this: The little kid in your life whose parents are struggling to make ends meet; they are waiting on you to FINISH. The college student you attend church with who is struggling to complete school; they need to witness you FINISH. The working professional you mentor who is struggling to advance in their career; they need to see your example how to FINISH. The key to another person's success is often connected and dependent on them having examples and role models in their lives, people that they actually know! Zing! Understanding this concept puts into perspective our goals and careers. This concept helps us understand that our personal achievement also contributes to greater societal good.

I have been a mentor to high school and college students since graduating college in 2008. A consistent theme I have seen is that many of these students have never seen a Black woman accountant, let alone a Black woman CPA. Students also do not always see the accounting profession as a viable option because they do not see people of color in leadership positions. I already mentioned the statistics of Black people represented in the well-recognized technical professionals (i.e., less than 2% Black CPAs and less than 5% Black doctors, engineers and lawyers). If we are going to increase those percentages, increasing representation of Black professionals, we have to persevere through both systemic external barriers and personal internal barriers. Thank God for organizations like the National Association of Black Accountants (NABA), the National Association of Black MBAs, the National Black Lawyers, the National

FINISH! *CONCLUSION*

Association of Black Engineers (NSBE) and even State Societies like the Indiana CPA Society. These organizations have consistent programming to visit high schools, mentor college students and provide professional development opportunities, all this to increase representation in their respective professions. They also advocate for diversity, equity, and inclusion, seeking to remove system barriers that prevent Black people from entering these professions and ones that cause them to leave the profession. It is my sincere hope that through our professional associations and our personal experiences, we continue to empower Black people and all people of color to advance professionally. That we show young people the opportunities available for them outside of sport, music, and art. That we continue to fight through our personal, and sometimes self-imposed, obstacles to reach our goals and advance professionally. We have to. For the culture. For our ancestors. For the future.

FINISH! *CONCLUSION*

For too long, the voices of Black people and other underrepresented and systemically oppressed people have been silenced. We have not been given the same opportunities to succeed. We have not been able to access the same level of power and influence. We have not been able to make a real difference in our communities and remove barriers in these predominately white professionals. If we quit now, our people will never see change.

Do not quit!

FINISH!

FINISH!

TOOLS

TOOLS

Keys Steps to Finish

1) Find a coach
2) Create a study group
3) Get a mentor
4) Add milestones to calendar
5) Let your job and family know

Add yours:

_____
_____
_____
_____
_____

TOOLS

Encouraging Notes to Self

1) Do not be afraid to be great!
2) If you don't like something, change it. If you can't change it, change your attitude
3) Do not be afraid to move forward in the purpose for which God has given you
4) It is okay to separate from anything and anyone who does not serve your purpose
5) Learn to love the process
6) Remember why you started
7) Remember your purpose and your goals
8) Don't let imposter syndrome and self-sabotage hold you back
9) Want it for yourself! No one can FINISH for you
10) It's not how you start, it's how you FINISH

Add yours:

_____
_____
_____
_____
_____
_____

TOOLS

Z's Zingers to remember

Zinger 1

_____

Zinger 2

_____

Zinger 3

_____

Zinger 4

_____

Zinger 5

_____

TOOLS

Zinger 6

_____

Zinger 7

_____

Zinger 8

_____

Zinger 9

_____

Zinger 10

_____

TOOLS

Personal Realizations

1. _____

2. _____

3. _____

4. _____

5. _____

6. _____

7. _____

8. _____

9. _____

10. _____

About the Author

E. ZeNai Brooks is a member of the underrepresented 2% of African-Americans who have accomplished the goal of obtaining the CPA license. She is a dynamic, millennial, business and community leader with over 13 years of professional experience. ZeNai has combined her passion for community advocacy and her professional career by having spent the latter of her public accounting career focusing on audits and consulting work within the not-for-profit industry. Currently, ZeNai serves as Controller of the Corporate Responsibility function of Cummins, a Fortune 200 Company and Treasurer of the related Foundation, which provides funding to grassroots initiatives and strategic programs around the world.

She is the wife of Darrell Brooks, Senior Pastor of the New Liberty Missionary Baptist Church in Indianapolis, IN. Her spiritual background is the foundation of her commitment to service, believing that we all have the responsibility to help others. ZeNai lives her life with purpose by using her knowledge and experiences to develop others and move the community forward. She believes that as we engage in community by giving back, empowering others and "Lifting as We Climb", everyone can make a difference! ZeNai is an example of a selfless person who leverages all her skills to change not only her life, but the lives of everyone she touches.

Inspirational Quote:

"When I stand before God at the end of my life, I would hope that I would not have a single bit of talent left, and could say, 'I used everything You gave me."
Chadwick Boseman

About ATKSP Firm

Order bulk books for your girls, women's groups, book club, professional organization, etc. @ www.drtuesday.net/shop. For individual orders, purchase via Amazon. Visit www.atkspf.com or email us @ atkspfirm@gmail.com, for more information on ATK Speakers and Publishing Firm; where we train and equip speaker to speak their truth and support authors in telling their story. For more information on the Executive Editor (Dr. Tuesday Tate) and to order other Author's books, visit her brand site @ www.drtuesday.net.

Made in the USA
Monee, IL
19 January 2025